Louisa May Alcott

Flower Fables

Illustrated by Leah Palmer Preiss

Stories compiled and edited by Daniel Shealy
Designed by Rymn Massand and Naomi Mizusaki

Okey-Doke Productions, Inc., New York

For my wonderful n&n's: Melanie, Ryan, Adina, Michael, Zach, and Tara. I followed my heart
in publishing this book, I hope they follow theirs in life.—With love, Kate

For the merry band of cousins: Caitlin, David, Genevieve, Max, Reed,
Robin, and Rosalia.—With love from Aunt Leah

This book is dedicated to my wife, Margaret, who also cherishes the tales of the fairy folk.—Daniel

For my father, your heart is the stuff of fables, and my mother,
your love of books is forever in me.—Christine

First edition
Printed in Toledo, Spain by Mondadori, D.L.TO: 90-1998

Published by Okey-Doke Productions, Inc.
49 West 55th Street, Suite 3R
New York, NY 10019

Distributed by Independent Publishers Group
814 North Franklin Street
Chicago, IL 60610
312.337.0747
800.888.4741

Publishing History
Flower Fables was originally published by George W. Briggs
of Boston in 1855. All of the six tales, with the exception
of "Little Annie's Dream:The Fairy Flower," were later
revised by Alcott and published by Roberts Brothers in
1887 as the second volume of Lulu's Library, entitled
The Frost King. "Ripple, the Water Sprite" was also published
in Merry's Museum in May 1870. Several "cheap" editions
of *Flower Fables* were reprinted in the late 19th and early
20th century. In 1992, all of the stories were published by
the University of Tennessee Press in Louisa May Alcott's
Fairy Tales and Fantasy Stories, a complete collection of Alcott's
fantasy fiction edited by Daniel Shealy. The texts for the
stories in this edition are taken from the revised 1887
The Frost King. "Little Annie's Dream:The Fairy Flower"
is from the original 1855 publication.

Library of Congress Catalog Card Number: 98-84386

ISBN 0-9660933-0-5

Contents

The summer moon shone brightly down upon the sleeping
earth while far away from mortal eyes danced the fairy folk.
Fireflies hung in bright clusters on the dewy leaves that waved
in the cool night wind. The flowers gazed in wonder at the little
elves who lay among the fern leaves, swung in the vine boughs,
and danced on the mossy ground to the music of bluebells,
ringing a merry peal in honor of the night.

Under the shade of a wild rose sat the Queen and her little elfin subjects
beside a silvery mushroom where a feast was spread.

"Now, my friends," said the Queen, "to while away the time till the bright
moon goes down, let us each tell a tale, or relate what we have done or
learned this day. I will begin with you, Sunnylock," she said, turning
to a lovely little elf lying among the fragrant leaves of a primrose.

With a gay smile, Sunnylock began her story.

"As I was painting the bright petals of a pansy,
it told me this tale. . . ."

The Frost King

The Queen sat upon her throne, and all the fairies from the four kingdoms were gathered for a grand council. A very important question was to be decided, and the bravest, wisest elves were meeting to see what could be done. The Frost King was making war upon the flowers, and it was a great grief to Queen Blossom and her subjects to see their darlings die year after year instead of enjoying one long summer, as they might have done but for him. She had sent messengers with splendid gifts and had begged him to stop this dreadful war, which made autumn so sad and left the fields strewn with dead flowers. But he sent back the gifts, sternly refused her prayers, and went on with his cruel work, because he was a tyrant and loved to destroy innocent things.

"My subjects, we will try once more," said the Queen. "Can anyone propose a plan that will touch his hard heart and make him kind to the dear flowers?"

There was a great rustling of wings and murmuring of voices, for all the elves were much excited, and each wanted to propose something. The Queen listened, but none of the plans seemed wise, and she was sadly perplexed. Then her favorite maid of honor, the lovely Star, came and knelt before her, saying, while her face shone and her voice trembled with the earnestness of her words, "Dear Queen, let me go alone to the Frost King and try what love will do. We have sent presents and prayers by messengers who feared and hated him, and he would not receive them, but we have not tried to make him love us, nor shown him how beautiful his land might be. We have not tried to patiently change that dreary place, to teach his people to plant flowers instead of killing them. I am not afraid. Let me go and try my plan, for love is very powerful, and I know he has a heart—if we can only find it."

"You may go, dear Star," answered the Queen, "and see if you can conquer him. But if any harm happens to you, we will come with our whole army and fight this cruel King till he is conquered."

At these brave words, all the elves cheered, and General Sun, the great warrior, waved his sword as if longing to go to battle at once. They gathered about Star, some to praise and caress her, some to warn her of the dangers of her task, others to tell her the way, and everyone to wish her success, for fairies are gentle little creatures and believe heartily in the power of love.

Star wished to go at once, so they wrapped her in a warm cloak of down from a swan's breast, gave her a bag of the seeds of all their sweetest flowers, and with kisses and tears went to the gates of Fairyland to say goodbye.

Smiling bravely, she flew away toward the north, where the frost spirits lived. Soon the wind grew cold, the sunshine faded, and snow began to fall, making Star shiver under her soft cloak. Presently she saw the King's palace. Pillars of ice held up the roof which was fringed with icicles that would have sparkled splendidly if there had been any sun. But all was dark and cold, and not a green leaf rustled or a bird sang in the wide plains, white with snow, that stretched as far as the eye could see. Before the doors stood the guards, frozen to their places, and they lifted their sharp spears and let Star go in when she said she was a messenger from the Queen.

Walls of ice carved with strange figures were round her, and carpets of snow covered the floor. On a throne hung with gray mist sat the King, a crown of crystals on his white hair, his mantle covered with silver frost. His eyes were cold and his face stern, and a smile never moved his hard lips. He frowned as he saw the fairy, and drew his cloak closer, as if afraid the light of her bright face might soften his heart.

Then Star told her errand, and in her gentle voice begged him to be kind. She described the sorrow of both elves and children when his frost killed all the flowers; she painted a bright picture of a world where it was always summer, and asked him to let her plant some flowers in his bleak fields, to show how lovely they made any spot.

But he only scowled and ordered her away, saying harshly, "I will do as I please, and if your Queen does not leave me in peace, I will go to war and freeze every fairy to death."

Star tried to say more, but he was so angry that he called his people and bid them shut her up till she would own that he was right and promise to let him kill all the flowers he liked.

"I will never do that," said Star, and the frost spirits led her away to a dark little cell and left her alone.

She was cold and tired and very sad that the King would not listen to her, but her heart was brave, and instead of crying, she began to sing. Soon the light of her own eyes, which shone like stars, made a little glimmer in the dark, and she saw that the floor of her cell was of earth. And presently she heard the tinkle of water as it dripped, drop by drop, down from the snow above. Then she smiled, so that it seemed as if a ray of light had crept in.

"Here is earth and water. I will make sunshine, and soon, by my fairy power, I will have a garden in Frostland." As she spoke, she pulled out the seeds and fell to work, singing, smiling, sure that in time she would do the hard task she had set herself. First she gathered the drops in her warm hands and moistened the hard earth; then she loosened it and planted her seeds along the walls; and then, sitting in the middle of the narrow room, she waved her wand and chanted the fairy spell that works the pretty miracle of turning seeds to flowers.

Sleep, little seed,
Deep in your bed,
While winter snow
Lies overhead.
Wake, little sprout,
And drink the rain,
Till sunshine calls
You to rise again.

Strike deep, young root,
In the earth below;
Unfold, pale leaves,
Begin to grow.
Baby bud, dance
In the warm sun;
Bloom, sweet rose,
Life has begun.

As she sang, the light grew stronger and the air warmer, and the drops fell like dew, till up came rows of little green vines and plants, growing like the magic beanstalk all over the walls and all round the room, making the once dark place look like an arbor. Moss spread like a carpet underfoot, and a silvery white mushroom sprung up beneath Star as if she were the queen of this pretty place.

Soon the frost spirits heard the music and went to see who dared sing in that gloomy prison. They were much surprised when they peered in, for instead of dying in her cell, the fairy had made it beautiful, and sat there singing while her flowers bloomed.

They hurried to the King and bade him come and see. He went, and when he saw the lovely place, he could not spoil it, for he wished to see what magic did such wonders. Now the dark walls were hung with morning glories, their many-colored bells ringing, and the floor was green with soft moss. The water drops made music as they fell, and rows of flowers nodded from their beds as if talking together in a sweet language of their own. Star sat on her throne, still singing and smiling, and the once dark place was as bright as if a little sun shone there.

"I am strong, but I cannot do that," said the King. "I love power, and perhaps if I watch, I shall learn some of her magic skill to use as I please. I will let her live, but keep her prisoner—and do as I please about killing other flowers."

So he left her there, but often stole down to peep, wondering at her cheerfulness and courage: though she longed for home, and found it very hard to be brave and patient, she never complained or cried.

Meanwhile, the Queen waited and waited for Star to come, and when a long time passed, she sent a messenger to learn her fate. The messenger brought back the sad tidings that she was a prisoner and that the King would not let her go. Then there was great weeping and wailing in Fairyland, for everyone loved gentle Star. They feared she would be frozen to death if they left her in the cruel King's power and resolved to go to war to set her free.

General Sun ordered out the army, and there was a great blowing of trumpets, beating of drums, and flying of flags as the little soldiers came marching from the four quarters of the kingdom. The earth elves were on foot, in green suits, with acorn cups for helmets and spear grass for lances. The water sprites were in blue armor made of dragonfly scales, and they drew shells full of tiny cannonball bubbles. The fire imps wore red and carried torches and little guns that fired brimstone. The air spirits were the finest of all, for they wore golden armor and carried arrows of light, which they shot from tiny rainbows. These came first, and General Sun was splendid to behold as he led them shining and flashing before the Queen, whose great banner of purple and gold streamed over their heads. The trumpets blew, the people cheered, and the elfin soldiers marched bravely away to fight the Frost King and bring Star home.

The Queen followed in a chariot drawn by white butterflies, with her maids and guards, the tallest elves in Fairyland. They lived in the pine trees and were fine strong fellows, with little cones on their heads, pine needles for swords, and the handsome russet scales for chain armor. Their shields were of sweet-smelling gum, like amber, and no one could approach the Queen when they made a wall about her, for whoever touched these shields stuck fast and was killed with the sharp swords.

Away streamed the army like a wandering rainbow, and by and by reached the land of frost and snow. The King had been warned that they were coming, and made ready by building a fort of ice, laying in piles of snowballs and arming his subjects with sharp icicles. All the cold winds that blow wailed like bagpipes, hailstones drummed on the frozen ground, and banners of mist floated over the towers of the palace. General Fog, in a suit of silver, stood ready to meet the enemy with an army of snowmen behind him, and the Frost King looked down from the walls to direct the fight.

On came the fairy folk, making the icy world sparkle so brilliantly with their light that the King was half-blinded and had to hide his eyes. The elves shivered as the cold wind touched them, but courage kept them warm, and the Queen, well wrapped in down, stood up in her chariot, boldly demanding Star from the King.

"I will not give her up," he answered, scowling like a thundercloud, though in his heart he wondered more and more how the brave fairy had lived so long away from such lovely friends as these.

"Then I proclaim war upon your country, and if Star is dead, we will show no mercy. Sound the trumpets and set on!" cried the Queen, waving her hand to the General. Every sword flashed out, and an elfin cheer rung like music in the air.

Ordering the rest to halt, General Sun led the air spirits to battle first, knowing well that nothing could stand long before a charge of that brilliant troop. General Fog did his best, but was driven back, for his snowmen melted away as the arrows of light struck them, and he could not stand before the other general, whose shield was a golden sun, without feeling himself dissolve like mist at noon.

They were forced to take refuge in the fort, where the King himself was ordering showers of snowballs to be shot among the fairy troops. Many were wounded, and were carried from the field to a tent where the Queen and her maids tended them and by their soft magic soon made them fit to fight again.

"Now, a grand attack," commanded General Sun. "Bring up the sappers and miners, Captain Rock. Major Flash, surround the walls and melt them as fast as possible."

Then a company of moles began to dig under the fort; the fire imps banged away at the walls with their cannon and held their flaming torches close, till the blocks of ice began to melt; the air spirits flew high above and shot their golden arrows down at the Frost people, who were dazzled and daunted by these brave and brilliant enemies, and fled to hide in the darkest corners.

It was a hard battle, and the fairies were obliged to rest after killing General Fog, destroying the fort, and forcing the King to take refuge in the palace. Among the prisoners taken was one who told them where Star was, and all she had done in her little cell. Then they rejoiced, and the Queen said, "Let us follow her example, for these prisoners say the King is changed since she came, that he goes to peep at her lovely garden and does not spoil it, but talks kindly to her; it seems as if his hard heart might be melting a little. We will not fight anymore, but try Star's gentle way and besiege the King till he surrenders. We shall win a friend, not kill an enemy."

"We will, we will!" cried all the elves, for though they were as brave as little lions in defending their country and their Queen, they did not love to fight. They all took counsel together, and the Frost people were surprised next day to see the army busily making a great garden round the palace. Creeping to the holes in the walls, they watched what went on and wondered more and more. The elves worked hard, and their magic helped them do in a day what would have taken mortals years.

First the moles dug up the ground, then the Queen's guard sowed pine seeds, and in an hour a green wall fenced in the garden. Then the earth fairies planted the seeds of all flowers that grow. The fire imps warmed the air and drove away the chilly wind, melting every gray cloud or flake of snow that dared come near this enchanted spot. The water sprites gathered drops from the melting ice palace and watered the budding beds, while the air spirits made sunshine overhead by flying to and fro with tireless wings, weaving a golden curtain that shut out the cold sky and made summer for the flowers.

The Queen and her maids helped by fashioning birds, bees, and butterflies with magic skill, and giving them life to sing, buzz, and flutter in the new world, where once all was bare and cold and dark.

Slowly the ice palace melted as warm airs stole through the pines, and soon the walls were thin as glass, the towers vanishing in the sun. Block after block flowed away in little streams, as if glad to escape from prison. The King and his subjects felt that they were conquered, for the ice seemed to melt from them also. Their hearts began to beat, their cold faces softened as if they wanted to smile, and they loved to watch and wonder at the sweet miracles the elves were working all about them.

The King tried not to give up, for he was very proud and had ruled for so long that it was hard to submit. But his power was gone: his palace was crumbling about him, his people longed to join the enemy, and there was nothing for him to do but lay down his crown or fly away to the far north and live with the bears and icebergs in that frozen world. He would have done this but for Star. All the while the battle and the siege were going on, she lived in her little cell, knowing nothing about it, but hoping and waiting, sure that help would come. Every time the King visited her, he seemed kinder, and liked more and more to listen to her songs or the stories she told him of life in Fairyland, of the joy of being merciful. So she knew that the seeds she sowed in his heart were beginning to grow like those planted in the cell, and she watched over them as carefully.

One day when her loveliest roses bloomed and she was singing for joy as the pink flowers filled the cell with their sweet breath, the King came hurrying down to her and, falling at her feet, begged her to save his life. She wondered what he meant, and then he told her of the battle, and of how the elves were conquering him by love. The palace was nearly gone, and a great garden lay blossoming all about it; he had nowhere to go unless she would be his friend and ask her people to forgive and pity him.

Then Star felt that she had done her task, and laying her hands on his white head, she melted the last frost from his old heart by saying in her tender voice, "Do not fear my people; they will welcome you and give you a home if you will promise to hurt no more flowers and always be as gentle as you are now. Come with me, and let us teach you how beautiful sunshine and love and happy work can make you."

The King promised, and Star led him up to the bright light, where his people waited to learn what was to become of them.

"Follow me, follow me, and do not be afraid," called Star, dancing before them, so glad to be free that she longed to fly away. Everything was changed; for as they came up from the cell, the ruins of the palace melted into a quiet lake, and under the archway of the pines, they passed into a new and lovely world of sunshine, flowers, and happy elves. A great cry went up when Star was seen leading the King, with his subjects behind him, and everyone flew to welcome the dear fairy and the captives she brought.

"I am your prisoner, and I submit, for I have no kingdom now," said the King, as he bowed before the Queen.

"These are the only chains you shall wear, and *this* is your new kingdom," answered the Queen, as her maids hung wreaths of flowers on the King's arms and put a green crown on his head. All the fairies gathered round to welcome him to the garden, where he was to reign beloved and happy, with no frost to spoil the long summer he had learned to love.

There was a great feast that day, and then the elfin army marched home again, well pleased with the battle they had fought, though all said that it was Star who had conquered the Frost King.

WHO LOVES A GARDEN STILL HIS EDEN KEEPS

BRONSON ALCOTT

Eva's Visit to Fairyland

As Sunnylock ceased, another little elf came forward, and this was the tale that Silverwing told. . . .

A little girl lay on the grass down by the brook wondering what the brown water said as it went babbling over the stones. As she listened, she heard another kind of music which seemed to come nearer and nearer, till round the corner floated a beautiful boat filled with elves, who danced on broad green leaves of lily of the valley. The white bells of the tall stem, which was the mast, rung loud and sweet.

A flat rock covered with moss stood in the middle of the brook, and here the boat was anchored for the elves to rest a little. Eva watched them at their play as they flew about or lay fanning themselves and drinking from red-brimmed cups on the rock. Wild strawberries grew in the grass close by, and Eva threw some of the ripest to the fairy folk, for honey and dew seemed a poor sort of lunch to the child. Then the elves saw her, and nodded and smiled and called, but their soft voices could not reach her. So after whispering among themselves, two of them flew to the brookside and, perching on a buttercup, said, close to Eva's ear, "We have come to thank you for your berries and to ask if we can do anything for you, because this is our holiday and we can become visible to you."

"Oh, let me go to Fairyland!" cried Eva. "I have longed to see and know all about you dear little people. I never believed it was true that there were no fairies left," she said, so glad to find that she was right.

"We should not dare to take some children, for they would do so much harm, but you believe in us. You love all the sweet things in the world and never hurt innocent creatures or tread on flowers, or let ugly passions come into your happy little heart. You shall go with us and see how we live."

But as the elves spoke, Eva looked very sad and said, "How can I go? I am so big— I should sink that pretty ship with one finger."

The elves laughed and touched her with their soft hands, saying, "You cannot hurt us now. Look in the water and see what we have done."

Eva looked and saw a tiny child standing under a tall blue violet. It was herself, in a white pinafore and little pink sunbonnet, but so small she seemed an elf. She clapped her hands and skipped for joy, but as she looked from the shore to the rock, she suddenly grew sober again.

"But now I am so wee, and I have no wings. I cannot step over, and you cannot lift me, I am sure."

"Give us each a hand, and do not be afraid," said the elves, and whisked her across like dandelion down.

The elves were very glad to see her and touched and peeped and asked questions as if they had never had a mortal child to play with before. Eva was so small that she could dance with them now and eat what they ate and sing their pretty songs. She found that flower-honey and dewdrops were very nice and that it was fine fun to tilt on a blade of grass, to slide down a smooth bulrush stem, or to rock in the cup of a flower. She learned new and merry games, found out what the brook said, saw a cowslip blossom, and had a lovely time, till the captain of the ship blew a long sweet blast on a honeysuckle horn and all the elves went aboard and set sail for home.

"Now I shall find the way to Fairyland and can go whenever I like," thought Eva, as she floated away.

But the sly little people did not wish her to know, for only now and then can a child go to that lovely place. So they set the bells to chiming softly, and all sung lullabies till Eva fell fast asleep, so that she would know nothing of the journey.

When she awoke in Fairyland, it seemed to be sunset, for the sky was red and the flowers were all dreaming behind their green curtains. The birds were tucked up in their nests and there was no sound but the whisper of the wind, which softly sang, "Goodnight, goodnight."

"We all go early to bed unless the moon shines," said the elves. "We are tired, so come and let us make you cozy till tomorrow." They showed her a dainty bed with white rose-leaves for sheets, a red rose-leaf for a coverlet, and two plump little mushrooms for pillows. Cobweb curtains hung over it, a glowworm was the candle, and a lily-of-the-valley cup made a nice nightcap, while a tiny gown of woven thistledown lay ready to be put on.

Eva quickly undressed and slipped into bed, where she lay looking at the red light till sleep kissed her eyelids. A lovely dream floated through her mind till morning came.

As soon as the sun peeped over the hills, the elves were up and away to the lake, where they all dipped and splashed and floated and frolicked till the air was full of sparkling drops and the water white with foam. Then they dried themselves with soft cobweb towels, which they spread on the grass to dry, and combed their hair and put on fresh gowns of flower petals. After that came breakfast: fruit and cakes of pollen, with fresh dew for drink.

"Now, Eva, you see that we are not idle, foolish creatures, but have many things to do, many lessons to learn, and a heaven of our own to hope for," said the elves. The wind, who was the housemaid there, cleared the tables by blowing everything away with one breath.

"First of all, come to our hospital, for here we bring all the sick and hurt things cruel or careless people have harmed. In your world, children often torment and kill poor birds and worms and flies, and pick flowers to throw away, and chase butterflies till their poor wings are broken. All these we care for, and our magic makes them live again. Come and see."

Eva followed to a cool, quiet place, where on soft beds lay many wounded things. Rose, the fairy nurse, was binding up the leg of a fly as he lay in a cobweb hammock and feebly buzzed his thanks. In another place an ugly worm was being put together after a cruel boy had cut him in two. Eva thought the elves were good to do such work, and went on to a hummingbird, which lay in a bed of honeysuckles, the quick colors very dim on its little breast and its bright wings very still.

"I was shot with an air gun, and my poor head still aches with the dreadful blow," sighed the poor bird, trying to sip a little honey with his long beak.

"I'm nearly well," chirped a cricket, whose stiff tail had been pulled off by a naughty child and nicely put on again by a very skillful elf.

He looked so cheerful and lively as he hopped about on his bed of dried grass, his black eyes twinkling and a bandage of bindweed holding his tail firmly in place till it was well. Eva laughed aloud, and at the pleasant sound, all the sick things smiled and seemed better.

Rows of pale flowers stood in one place, and elves watered them or tied up broken leaves or let in the sunshine to cure their pains, for these delicate invalids needed much care. Mignonette was the name of the nurse who watched over them, like a little Sister of Charity, with her gray gown and sweet face.

"You have seen enough. Come to school now and see where we are taught all that fairies must know," said Trip, the elf who was guiding her about.

In a pleasant place, they found the child elves sitting on pink daisies with their books of leaves in their hands. The teacher, a jack-in-the-pulpit, asked questions and was very wise. Eva nodded to the little ones, and they smiled at the stranger as they rustled their books and pretended to study busily.

A class in arithmetic was going on, and Eva listened to questions that none but elves would care to know.

"Twinkle, if there were fifteen seeds on a dandelion, and the wind blew ten away, how many would be left?"

"Five."

"Bud, if a rose opens three leaves one day, two the next, and seven the next, how many in all?"

"Twelve."

"Daisy, if a silkworm spins one yard of fairy cloth in an hour, how many can he spin in a day?"

"Twelve, if he isn't lazy," answered the little elf, fluttering her wings as if anxious to be done.

"Now we will read," said the jack-in-the-pulpit, and the class flew to the long leaf, where they stood in a row, with books open, ready to begin.

"You may read 'The Flower's Lesson' today, and be careful not to singsong, Poppy," said the teacher, passing a dainty book to Eva, so that she could follow the story.

"Once there was a rose who had two little buds. One was happy and contented, but the other always wanted something.

" 'I wish the elves would bring me a star instead of dew every night. The drop is soon gone, but a star would shine splendidly, and I should be finer than all the other flowers,' said the naughty bud one night.

" 'But you need the dew to live, and the moon needs the stars up there to light the world. Don't fret, sister, but be sure it is best to take what is sent, and be glad,' answered the good bud.

" 'I won't have the dew, and if I cannot get a star, I will take a firefly to shine on my breast,' said the other, shaking off a fresh drop that had just fallen on her and folding her leaves round the bright fly.

" 'Foolish child!' cried the rose-mother. 'Let the fly go before he harms you. It is better to be sweet and fair than to shine with a beauty not your own. Be wise, dear, before it is too late.'

"But the silly bud only held the firefly closer, till in its struggles it tore her leaves and flew away. When the hot sun came up, the poor bud hung all faded on her stem, longing for a cool drop to drink. Her sister was strong and fresh and danced gaily in the wind, opening her red petals to the sun.

" 'Now I must die. Oh, why was I vain and silly?' sobbed the poor bud, fainting in the heat.

"Then the mother leaned over her, and from her bosom, where she had hidden it, the dewdrop fell on the thirsty bud. And while she drank it eagerly, the rose drew her closer, whispering, 'Little darling, learn to be contented with what heaven sends, and make yourself lovely by being good.'"

"I shall remember that story," said Eva when the elves shut their books and flew back to the daisy seats.

"Would you like to hear them sing?" asked Trip.

"Very much," said Eva, and in the little song they gave her, she got another lesson to carry home.

"I shine," says the sun,
"To give the world light."
"I glimmer," adds the moon,
"To beautify the night."
"I ripple," says the brook,
"I whisper," sighs the breeze,
"I patter," laughs the rain,
"We rustle," call the trees.

"We dance," nod the daisies,
"I twinkle," shines the star,
"We sing," chant the birds,
"How happy we all are!"
"I smile," cries the child,
Gentle, good, and gay.
The sweetest thing of all,
The sunshine of each day.

"I shall sing that to myself and try to do my part," said Eva as the elves got out their paints and brushes of butterfly down and, using large white leaves for paper, learned to imitate the colors of every flower.

"Why do they do this?" asked Eva, for she saw no pictures anywhere. "We keep the flowers fresh, for in the world below, they have trials with the hot sun that fades, the mold that spots, the grubs that gnaw, and the frost that kills. We melt bits of rainbow in our paint pots, and when it is needed, we brighten the soft color on Anemone's cheeks, deepen the blue of Violet's eyes, or polish up the cowslips till they shine like cups of gold. We redden the autumn leaves and put the purple bloom on the grapes. We make the budding birches a soft green, color maple keys, and hang brown tassels on the alder twigs. We repair the dim spots on butterflies' wings, paint the bluebird like the sky, give Robin his red vest, and turn the yellow bird to a flash of sunshine. Oh, we are artists, and hereafter you will see our pictures everywhere."

"How lovely!" said Eva. "I often wondered who kept all these delicate things so beautiful and gay. But where are we going now?" she added, as the elves led her away from the school.

"Come and see where we learn to ride," they answered, smiling as if they enjoyed this part of their education.

In a little dell, where the ground was covered with the softest moss, Eva found the fairy riding-school and gymnasium. The horses were all kinds of winged and swift-footed things, and the racetrack was a smooth path round the highest mound. Groups of elves lay on the ground, swung on the grass blades, or sat in the wood flowers that stood all about.

In one place, the mothers and fathers were teaching their little ones to fly. The baby elves sat in a row on the branch of a birch tree, fluttering their small wings and nestling close together, timid yet longing to launch boldly out into the air and float as the others did. The parents were very patient, and one by one the babies took little flights, getting braver and braver each time.

One very timid elf would not stir, so the sly papa and mama put it on a leaf, and each taking a side, they rode the dear about for a few minutes, till she was used to the motion. Then they dropped the leaf, and the little elf, finding herself falling, spread her wings and flew away to a tall bush—to the great delight of all who saw it.

But the riding was very funny, and Eva soon forgot everything else in watching the gay creatures mount their various horses and fly or gallop round the ring while the teacher—a small fellow in a cap and green suit—stood on the mound of moss, cracking a long whip and telling them how to ride in the best fairy fashion.

Several lady elves learned to mount butterflies gracefully and float where they liked, sitting firmly when the winged horses alighted

on the flowers. The boy elves preferred field mice, sitting on saddles of woven grass and using reins of yellow bindweed, which looked fine on the little gray creatures, who went very swiftly round and round, twinkling their bright eyes and whisking their long tails as if they liked it.

But the best fun of all was when the leaping began. Grasshoppers were led out, and the gallant elves leaped over the highest flowers without falling off. It was very funny to see the hoppers skipping with their long legs. When Puck, the riding master, mounted and led a dozen of his pupils on a race round the track, all the rest of the elves laughed aloud and clapped their hands with glee, for Puck was a famous fairy, and his pranks were endless.

Eva was shouting with the rest as the green horses came hopping by, and Puck caught her up before him. Away they raced, so swiftly that her hair whistled in the wind and her breath was nearly gone. A tremendous leap took them high over the hill and landed Eva in a tall dandelion, where she lay laughing and panting as if on a little yellow sofa, and Trip and her mates fanned her and smoothed her hair.

"That was splendid!" she cried. "I wish I was a real fairy and always lived in this lovely place. Everything will seem so ugly and big and coarse when I go home. I shall never be happy again."

"Oh, yes, you will," answered Trip, "for after this visit, you will be able to hear and see and know what others never do, and that will make you happy and good. You believed in us, and we reward all who love what we love, and enjoy the beautiful world they live in as we do."

"Thank you," said Eva. "If I can know what the birds sing and the brook babbles, and can talk with the flowers and see faces in the sky and hear music in the wind, I won't mind being a child, even if people call me queer."

"You shall understand many lovely things and be able to put them into tales and songs that all will read and sing and thank you for," said Moonbeam, a sweet, thoughtful elf who stole quietly about and was always singing like a soft wind.

"Oh, that is what I always wanted to do," cried Eva, "for I love my songbooks best and never find new ones enough. Show me more, dear elves, so that I can have many fine tales to tell when I am old enough to write."

"Come, then, and see our sweetest sight. We cannot show it to everyone, but your eyes will be able to see through the veil, and you will understand the meaning of our flower heaven."

So Moonbeam led her away from all the rest, along a little winding path that went higher and higher, till they stood on a hilltop.

"Look up and follow me," said the elf, and touching Eva's shoulders with her wand, a pair of wings shot out, and away she floated after her guide, toward what looked like a white cloud sailing in the blue sky.

When they alighted, a soft mist was round them, and through it Eva saw a golden glimmer like sunshine.

"Look, but do not speak," said Moonbeam, beckoning her along.

Soon the mist passed away, and nothing but a thin veil of gossamer, like a silken cobweb, hung between them and the world beyond. "Can you see through it?" whispered the elf anxiously.

Eva nodded and then forgot everything as she looked with all her sight into a lovely land of flowers. The walls were of white lilies, the trees rose trees, the ground blue violets, and the birds a little plant whose blossoms are like hummingbirds in flight. Columbines sounded their red horns, and the air was filled with delicate voices unlike any ever heard before: it was the sweet breath of flowers set to music.

But what surprised Eva most was the sight of a common dandelion, a tuft of clover, a faded mignonette, and several other humble flowers. They were set in a little plot by themselves, and about them gathered a crowd of beautiful spirits, so bright, so small, so perfect that Eva could hardly see them. She winked as if dazzled by the sunshine of this garden among the clouds.

"Who are they? And why do they care for those poor flowers?" whispered Eva, forgetting that she must not speak.

Before Moonbeam could answer, all grew dim for a moment, as if a cold breath had passed beyond the curtain and chilled the delicate world within.

"Hush! Mortal voices must not be heard here," answered the elf with a warning look.

"These lovely creatures are the spirits of flowers who did some good deed when they bloomed on earth, and their reward is to live here forever, where there is no frost, no rain, no stormy wind to hurt them. Those poor plants have just come, for their work is done and their souls will soon be set free from the shapes that hold them. You will see how beautiful they have made themselves when out of the common flowers come souls like the perfect ones who are welcoming them.

"That dandelion lived in the room of a poor little sick girl who had no other toy, no other playmate. She watched and loved it as she lay on her bed, for she was never well, and the good flower, instead of fading without sunshine in that dreary room, bloomed its best, till it shone like a little sun. The child died with it in her hand, and when she no longer needed it, we saved it from being thrown away and brought it here to live forever.

"The clover grew in a prison yard, and a bad boy shut up there watched it. It was the only green thing there, and it made him think of the fields at home, where his mother was waiting and hoping he would come back to her. Clover did her best to keep good thoughts in his mind, and he loved her and tried to repent, and when he was told he might go, he meant to take his flower with him, but forgot it in his hurry to get home. We did not forget, for the wind, which goes everywhere, had told us the little story, and we brought brave Clover out of prison to this flower heaven.

"Mignonette lived in a splendid garden, but no one minded her, for she is only a little brown thing. She hid in a corner, happy with her share of sunshine and rain and her daily task of blossoming green and strong. People admired the other fine flowers and praised their perfume, never knowing that the sweetest breath of all came from the nook where Mignonette modestly hid behind the roses. No one ever praised her or came to watch her. But the bees found her out and came every day to sip her sweet honey. The butterflies loved her better than the proud roses, and the wind always stopped for a kiss as it flew by. When autumn came, and all the other plants, their blossoming done, stood bare and faded, modest Mignonette stood, still green and fresh, still with a blossom or two, and still smiling contentedly with a bosom full of ripened seeds, her summer work well done, her happy heart ready for the winter sleep.

"But we said, 'No frost shall touch our brave flower; she shall not be neglected another year but will come to live loved and honored in the eternal summer that shines here.' Now look."

Eva brushed away the tears that had filled her eyes as she listened to these little histories, and looking eagerly, saw how, set free by the spells the spirits sang, there rose from the dandelion a little golden soul in the delicate shape the others wore. One in pale rose came from the clover, and a bright face flew out of the mignonette. Then the others took hands and floated round the newcomers in an airy dance, singing so joyfully that Eva clapped her hands, crying, "Happy souls!

I will go home and try to be as good as they were; then I may be as happy when I go away to my heaven."

The sound of her voice made all dark, and she would have been frightened if the elf had not taken her hand and led her back to the edge of the cloud, saying as they flew down to Fairyland, "See, the sun is setting; we must take you home before this midsummer day ends, and with it our power to make ourselves known."

Eva had so much to tell that she was ready to go, but a new surprise waited for her when she came again to Fairyland.

Banners of gay tulip leaves were blowing in the wind from the lances of reeds held by a troop of elves mounted on mice; a car made of a curled green leaf with checkerberry wheels and cushions of pink mushrooms stood ready for her, and Trip, as maid of honor, helped her in. Lady elves on butterflies flew behind, and the Queen's trumpeters marched before, making music on their horns. All the people of Fairyland lined the way, throwing flowers, waving their hands, and calling, "Farewell, little Eva! Come again! Do not forget us!" till she was out of sight.

"How sweet and kind you are to me. What can I do to thank you?" Eva asked Trip, who sat beside her as they rolled along.

"Remember all you have seen and heard. Love the good and beautiful things you will find everywhere, and be always a happy child at heart," answered Trip with a kiss.

Before Eva could speak, the sun set. In a moment, every elf was invisible. All the pretty show was gone, and the child stood alone by the brook. But she never forgot her visit to Fairyland, and as she grew up, she seemed to be a sort of elf herself: happy, gay, and good, with the power of making everyone love her as she went singing and smiling through the world. She wrote songs that people loved to sing, told tales children delighted to read, and found so much wisdom, beauty, and music everywhere that it was very plain she understood the sweet language of bird and flower, of wind and water, and that she remembered all the lessons the elves taught her.

Lilybell and Thistledown

"You shall come next, Zephyr," said the Queen. And the little fairy, who lay rocking to and fro upon a fluttering vine leaf, thus began her story. . . .

Once upon a time, two little fairies went out into the world to seek their fortune. Thistledown wore a green suit, a purple cloak, and a gay feather in his cap, and was as handsome an elf as one could wish to see. But he was not loved in Fairyland, for like the flower whose name and colors he wore, many faults were hidden like sharp prickles under his fine clothes. He was idle, selfish, and cruel, and cared for nothing but his own pleasure and comfort, as we shall see.

His little friend Lilybell was very different, for she was kind and good, and everyone loved her. She spent her time trying to undo the mischief naughty Thistle did, and that was why she followed him now, because she was afraid he would get into trouble and need someone to help him.

Side by side they flew over hill and dale till they came to a pleasant garden. "I am tired and hungry," said Thistle. "Let us rest here and see what fun is going on."

"Now, dear Thistle, be kind and gentle, and make friends among these flowers. See how they spread their leaves for our beds and offer us their honey to eat and their dew to bathe in. It would be very wrong to treat them badly after such a welcome as this," answered Lilybell, as she lay down to sleep in the deep cup of a flower, as if in a little bed hung with white curtains.

Thistle laughed and flew off to find the tulips, for he liked splendid flowers and lived like a king. First he robbed the violets of their honey and shook the bluebells roughly to get all their dew for his bath. Then he ruffled many leaves to make a bed that suited him, and after a short nap he was up and away having what he called fun. He chased the butterflies and hurt them with the sharp thorn he carried for a sword; he broke the cobwebs laid to bleach on the grass for fairy cloth; he pushed the little birds out of the nest; he stole pollen from the busy bees and laughed to see them patiently begin to fill their little bags again. At last he came to a lovely rose tree with one open flower and a little bud.

"Why are you so slow about blooming, baby rose? You are too old to be rocked in your green cradle any longer. Come out and play with me," said Thistle, as he perched on the tree ready for more mischief.

"No, my little bud is not strong enough to meet the sun and air yet," answered the rose-mother, bending over her baby, all her red leaves trembling with fear, because the wind had told her the harm this cruel fairy had been doing in the garden.

"You're a silly flower to wait so long. See how quickly I will make the ugly green bud a pretty pink rose," cried Thistle, and he pulled open the folded bud so rudely that the little leaves fell all broken on the ground.

"It was my first and only one, and I was so fond and proud of it! Now you have killed it, cruel fairy, and I am all alone," sobbed the mother, her tears falling like rain on the poor bud fading in the hot sun.

Thistle was ashamed of himself, but he would not say he was sorry, and flew away to hunt a white moth till clouds began to gather and a shower came on. Then he hurried back to the tulips for shelter, sure they would take him in because he had praised their gay colors, and they were vain flowers. But when he came all wet and cold, begging to be covered, they laughed and shook their broad leaves till the drops fell on him faster than the rain and beat him down.

"Go away, naughty fairy! We know you now, and won't let you in, for you bring trouble wherever you go. You needn't come to us for a new cloak when the shower has spoilt that one," they cried.

"I don't care. The daisies will be glad to take pity on so splendid an elf as I am," said Thistle, and he flew down to the humble flowers in the grass.

But all the rosy leaves were tightly closed, and he knocked in vain, for the daisies had heard of his pranks and would not risk spoiling their seeds by opening to such a rascal.

He tried the buttercups and dandelions, the violets and mignonettes, the lilies and the honeysuckles, but all shut their doors against him and told him to go away.

"Now I have no friends and must die of cold. If I had only minded Lilybell I might be safe and warm as she is somewhere," sighed Thistle, as he stood shivering in the rain.

"I have no little bud to shelter now, and you can come in here," said a soft voice above him. Looking up, Thistle saw that he was under the rose tree, where the dead bud hung broken on its stem.

Grieved and ashamed, the fairy gladly crept in among the warm red leaves, and the rose-mother held him close to her gentle bosom, where no rain or chilly wind could reach him. But when she thought he was asleep, she sighed so sadly over her lost baby that Thistle found no rest and dreamed only sad dreams.

Soon the sun shone again and Lilybell came to find her friend, but he was ashamed to meet her and stole away. When the flowers told Lily all the harm Thistle had done, she was very sorrowful and tried to comfort them. She cured the hurt birds and butterflies, helped the bees he had robbed, and watered the poor rose till more buds came to bloom on her stem. Then when all were well and happy again, she went to find Thistle, leaving the garden full of grateful friends.

Meanwhile, Thistle had been playing more pranks and had gotten into more trouble. A kind bee invited him to dinner one day, and the fairy liked the pretty home in the hive: the floors were of white wax, the walls of golden honeycomb, and the air sweet with the breath of flowers. It was a busy place; some got the food and stored it up in the little cells; some were the housemaids, and kept all exquisitely neat; some took care of the eggs and fed the young bees like good nurses; and others waited on the Queen.

"Will you stay and work with us? No one is idle here, and it is a happier life than playing all day," said Buzz, the friendly bee.

"I hate to work," answered lazy Thistle, and would not do anything at all.

When they told him that he must go he became angry and he went to some of the bees whom he had made discontented by his fine tales of an idle life, and he said to them, "Let us feast and be jolly; winter is far off and there is no need to work in the summertime. Come and make merry while those busy fellows are away and the nurses are watching the babies in the cells."

Then he led the drones to the hive like a band of robbers. First they locked the

Queen in her royal room so she could do nothing but buzz angrily. Next they drove the poor housekeepers away and frightened the little bees into fits as they rioted through the waxen halls, pulling down the honeycomb and stealing the bee-bread carefully put away in the neat cells for wintertime. They stayed as long as they dared, then flew off before the workers came home to find their pretty hive in ruins.

"That was fine fun," said Thistle as he went to hide in a great forest where he thought the angry bees could not find him.

Here he soon made friends with Gauzy-wing, a gay dragonfly, and they had splendid games skimming over the lake or swinging on the ferns that grew about it. For a while Thistle was good, and he might have had a happy time if he had not quarreled with his friend about a little fish that the cruel elf had pricked with his sword till it nearly died. Gauzy-wing thought that very cruel and said he would tell the Brownies, who ruled over everything in the wood.

"I'm not afraid," answered Thistle. "They can't hurt me."

But he *was* afraid, and as soon as the dragonfly was asleep that night, he got an ugly spider to come and spin webs all round the poor thing, till it could stir neither leg nor wing.

Leaving Gauzy-wing to starve, Thistle flew out of the wood, sure that the Brownies would not catch him.

But they did, for they knew all that happened in their kingdom, and when Thistle stopped to rest in a wild morning-glory bell, they sent word by the wind that he was to be kept a prisoner till they came. So the purple leaves closed round the sleeping fairy, and he woke to find himself held fast. Then he knew how poor Gauzy-wing felt and wished he had not been so unkind. But it was too late, for soon the Brownies came, and tying his wings with a strong blade of grass, they said as they led him away, "You do so much harm that we are going to keep you a prisoner till you repent, for no one can live in this beautiful world unless he is kind and good. Here you will have time to think over your naughtiness and learn to be a better elf."

So they shut him up in a great rock where there was no light except for one little ray through a crack that let air into his narrow cell, and there poor Thistle sat alone, longing to be free and sobbing over all the pleasant things he had lost. By and by, he stopped crying, and said to himself, "Perhaps if I am patient and cheerful, even in this dark place, the Brownies will let me out." So he began to sing, and the more he sang, the better he felt, for the ray of sunshine seemed to grow brighter, the days shorter, and his sorrow easier to bear.

Lilybell was looking for him all this time, tracing him by the harm he had done and stopping to comfort those whom he had hurt. Only after she had helped the bees put the hive in order, set free poor Gauzy-wing, and nursed the hurt fish till it was well again could she go on looking for him. She never would have found him if he had not sung so much, for the birds loved to hear him and often perched on the rocks to listen and learn the fairy songs. Columbines sprung up there in the sunshine and danced on their slender stems as they peeped in at him with rosy faces, and green moss went creeping up the sides of the rock as if eager to join in the music.

As Lilybell came to this pleasant place, she wondered if there was a fairy party going on, for the birds were singing, the flowers dancing, and the old rock looked very gay. When they saw her, the birds stopped and the columbines stood so still that she heard a voice singing sadly,

Bright shines the summer sun,
Soft is the summer air,
Gaily the wood birds sing,
Flowers are blooming fair.
But deep in the dark, cold rock
All alone must I dwell,
Longing for you, dear friend,
Lilybell, Lilybell!

"Where are you?" cried Lilybell, flying up among the columbines. She could see no opening in the rock, and no one replied, for Thistle did not hear her, so she sang her answer to his call,

Through sunshine and shower
I have looked for you long,
Guided by bird and flower,
And now by your song,
Thistledown! Thistledown!
O'er wood, hill, and dell
Hither to comfort you
Comes Lilybell.

Then, through the narrow opening, two arms were stretched out to her, and all the columbines danced for joy that Thistle was found.

Lilybell made her home there, and did all she could to cheer the poor prisoner, glad to see that he was sorry for his naughtiness and really trying to be good. But he pined so to come out that she could not bear it and said she would go and ask the Brownies what he could do to be free.

Thistle waited and waited, but she did not come back, and he cried and called so pitifully that the Brownies came at last and took him out, saying, "Lilybell is safe, but she is in a magic sleep and will not wake till you bring us a golden wand from the earth elves, a cloak of sunshine from the air spirits, and a crown of diamonds from the water fairies. It is a hard task, for you have no friends to help you along. But if you love Lilybell enough to be patient, brave, and kind, you may succeed, and she will wake to reward you when you bring the fairy gifts."

As they said this, the Brownies led him to a green tent made of tall ferns, and inside on a bed of moss lay Lilybell fast asleep.

"I will do it," said Thistle, and spreading the wings that had been idle so long, he was off like a hummingbird.

"Flowers know most about the earth elves, so I will ask them," he thought, and began to ask every clover, buttercup, wood violet, and wayside dandelion that he met. But no one would answer him; all shrunk away and drew their curtains close, remembering his rough treatment before.

"I will go to the rose. I think she is a friend, for she forgave me and took me in when the rest left me in the cold," said Thistle, much discouraged and half afraid to ask anything of the flower he had hurt so much.

But when he came to the garden, the rose-mother welcomed him kindly and proudly showed the family of little buds that now grew on her stem.

"I will trust and help you for Lilybell's sake," she said. "Look up, my darlings, and show the friend how rosy your little faces are growing; you need not be afraid now."

But the buds leaned closer to their mother and would only peep at Thistle, for they remembered the little sister whom he had killed and they feared him.

"Ah," he sadly thought, "if I had only been kind like Lily, they would all love and trust me and be glad to help me. How beautiful goodness is! I must try to prove to them that I am sorry; then they will believe me and show me how to find the crown."

So at night, when the flowers were asleep, he watered them. He sang lullabies to the restless young birds and tucked the butterflies up under the leaves where no dew could spoil their lovely wings. He rocked the baby buds to sleep when they grew impatient to blossom. He kept grubs from harming the delicate leaves of the flowers and brought cool winds to refresh them when the sun was hot.

The rose was always good to him, and when the other plants wondered who did so many kind things, she said to them, "It is Thistle, and he is so changed that I am sure we may trust him. He hides by day, for no one is friendly, but by night he works or sits alone and sobs and sighs so sadly that I cannot sleep for pity."

Then they all answered, "We will love and help him for Lilybell's sake."

So they called him to come and be friends, and he was very happy to be forgiven. But he did not forget his task, and when he told them what it was, they called Downy-back, the mole, and bid him show Thistle where the earth elves lived. Thanking the kind flowers, Thistle followed the mole deep into the ground, along the road Downy-back knew so well, till they saw a light before them.

"There they are. Now you can go on alone, and good luck to you," said Downy-back as he scampered away—for he liked the dark best.

Thistle came to a great hall made of jewels that shone like the sun, and here many spirits were dancing like fireflies to the music of silver bells.

One of these came and asked why he was there, and when he told her, Sparkle said, "You must work for us if you want to earn the golden wand."

"What must I do?" asked Thistle. "Many things," answered Sparkle. "Some of us watch over the roots of the flowers and keep them warm and safe; others gather drops and make springs that gush up among the rocks, where people drink the fresh water and are glad; others dig for jewels, make good-luck pennies, and help miners find gold and silver hidden in dark places. Can you be happy here, and do all these things faithfully?"

"Yes, for the love of Lily I can do anything," said Thistle bravely, and he fell to work at once with all his heart.

It was hard and dull for the gay fairy, who loved light and air, to live in the earth like a mole, and often he was very sad and tired, and longed to fly away to rest. But he never did, and at last Sparkle said, "You have done enough. Here is the golden wand and as many jewels as you like."

But Thistle cared only for the wand, and hurried up to the sunshine as fast as he could climb, eager to show the Brownies how well he had kept his word.

They were very glad to see him back and told him to rest a little. But he could not wait, and with a look at Lily, still fast asleep, he flew away to find the air spirits.

No one seemed to know where they lived, and Thistle was in despair till he remembered hearing Buzz, the friendly bee, speak of them when he first met him.

"I dare not go to the hive, for the bees might kill me for doing so much harm. Perhaps if I first show them I am sorry they will forgive me as the flowers did," he thought.

So he went into the field of clover and worked busily till he had filled two bluebells with the sweetest honey. These he left at the door of the hive when no one saw him, and then hid in an appletree close by.

The bees were much pleased and surprised with the two little blue jars at the door, full of honey so fresh and sweet that it was kept for the Queen and the royal babies.

"It is some good elf who knows how much trouble we have had this summer and wants to help us fill our cells before the frost comes. If we catch the kind fellow, we will thank him well," said the bees gratefully.

"Aha! we shall be friends again, I think, if I keep on," laughed Thistle, much cheered as he sat among the leaves.

Everyday after this he not only left the pretty honey pots but flew far and wide for all the flowering herbs bees love to suck, nearly breaking his back lugging berries from the wood, and great bags of pollen for their bread. He helped the ants with their heavy loads and the field mice with their small harvesting, and he chased flies from the patient cows feeding in the fields. No one saw him, but all loved "Nimble Nobody," as they called the invisible friend who did so many kindly things.

At last they caught him, as he was wrapping a lizard who had chills in a warm mullein-leaf blanket.

"Why, it is naughty Thistle!" cried the bees, ready to sting him to death.

"No, no," chirped an old cricket who had seen Thistle's good deeds and kept the secret. "It is the good fellow who has done so much to make us all happy and comfortable. Put up your stings and shake hands before he flies away to hide from you again."

The bees could hardly believe this at first, but finding it true, they were glad to make up and be friends. When they heard what Thistle wanted, they consented at once, and sent Buzz to show him the way to Cloudland, where the air spirits lived.

Cloudland seemed a lovely place, for the sky was gold and purple overhead, silver mist hung like curtains from the rainbow arches, and white clouds were piled up like downy cushions for the spirits to sleep on. But the air spirits were very busy, flying to and fro like motes in a sunbeam, some polishing the stars that they might shine well at night, some drawing up water from rivers and lakes to shower it down again in rain or dew. Still more air spirits were busy sending messages on the winds that kept coming and going like telegraph boys, carrying news to all parts of the world. And others were weaving light into a shiny material that they hung on dark walls, wrapped about budding plants, and clothed all spirits of the airy world with.

"These are the ones I want," said Thistle, and asked for the mantle of sunshine.

"You must earn it first, by helping us work," said the weavers.

Thistle willingly went with them and shared their lovely tasks, but most of all he liked to shake sweet dreams from the dreamland tree down upon little people in their beds, and to send strong, bright rays into dark rooms, so that they danced on walls and cheered sick or sad eyes. Sometimes he went riding to the earth on a raindrop, like a little water-cart man, and sprinkled the dusty road or gave some thirsty plant a good drink. He helped the winds carry messages and blow flower seeds into lonely places to spring and blossom there, a pleasant surprise for any who might find them.

It was a busy and happy life, and he liked it, for fairies love light, air, and motion, and he was learning to live for good and helpful things. Sooner than he expected, the golden cloak was won, and he shot like a falling star to the forest with his prize.

"One more trial and she will wake," said the Brownies, well pleased.

"This I shall not like, for I am not a water elf, but I'll do my best," answered Thistle, and he roamed away into the woods to look for the crown of diamonds, following a brook till he came to the lake where he used to play with Gauzy-wing. As he stood wondering how to find the water fairies, he heard a faint cry for help and presently found a little frog with a broken leg lying on the moss.

"I tried to jump too far when a cruel child was going to tread on me, and fell among the stones. I long for the water but can drag myself no farther," sighed the frog, his bright eyes dim with pain.

Thistle did not like to touch the cold thing. But remembering his own unkindness to the dragonfly, he helped Hop—for this was the poor froggie's name—to a fallen oak leaf, which he then tugged by its stout stem to the waterside, where he could bathe the hurt leg and bring the frog cool drafts in an acorn cup.

"Alas! I cannot swim, and I am very tired of this bed," cried Hop after a day or two, during which Thistle fed and nursed him tenderly.

"I'll pull a lily pad to the shore, and when you are on it we can sail about wherever we please without tiring you," said Thistle, and away he went to find the green boat.

After that, they floated all day and anchored at night, until Hop was well enough to dive off and paddle a bit with his hands or float using his good leg to steer with. Thistle had talked about the water fairies, but Hop was rather a dull fellow who lived in the mud, so he could tell him nothing. One day, however, a little fish popped up his head and said, "I know, and for kind Lilybell's sake I'll show you where they live."

Then Thistle left grateful Hop to his family and, folding his wings, plunged into the lake after the silvery fish, who darted deeper and deeper till they stood in a curious palace made of rosy coral at the bottom of the sea. Gay shells made the floors and ornamented the walls. Lovely seaweed grew from the white sand, and heaps of pearls lay everywhere. The water fairies in their blue robes floated here and there or slept in beds of foam, rocked by the motion of the waves.

They gathered round the stranger, bringing all sorts of treasures for him. But he did not care for these, and told them what he wanted.

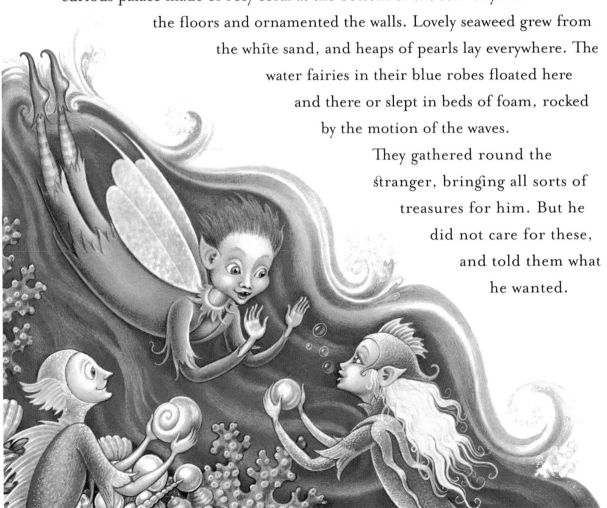

Then little Pearl, the gentlest of the sprites, said, "You must help the coral-workers till the branches of their tree reach the air. We want a new island, and that is the way we begin them. It is very dull work, but we cannot give you the crown till that is done."

Thistle was ready to begin at once and hastened away to the coral tree, where hundreds of little creatures were building cell upon cell. It was very dull, and the poor fairy never could lose his fear of the strange monsters that swam to and fro, staring at him with big eyes, or opening their great mouths as if to swallow him. There was no sun, only a dim light, and the sky seemed full of storm. Waves rolled overhead, and wrecks came floating down. The sea flowers had no sweetness, and the only birds were flying fish and Mother Carey's chickens, as the stormy petrels are called. Thistle pined for light and air but kept patiently at work. His only pleasure was now and then to float with Pearl on the waves that rippled to the shore and get a breath of warm air from the lovely earth he longed to see again.

At last the great tree rose tall and wide, spreading through the blue water and above the sea. Now the waves would wash weeds over the branches, gulls would bring earth and sticks to make their nests, and by and by an island would be formed where men might land or wild birds live in peace.

"Now you can go. Here is the crown of waterdrop diamonds, which will always lie cool and bright on your Lily's head. Goodbye, goodbye," said Pearl as she gave the reward and waved her hand to Thistle, who shook the foam off his wings and flew away in the sunshine like a happy butterfly just out of its cell.

When he came to the wood, the Brownies hastened to meet him, and he saw that they had made the place beautiful with wreaths hanging from each tree. Birds were singing their sweetest on every bough, and the brook was laughing as it hurried by to tell the good news wherever it went. The flowers, all in their best, were dancing with impatience to welcome him home.

Lilybell lay with the cloak of sunshine folded round her and the golden wand in her hand, waiting for the crown and the kiss that should wake her from this long sleep. Thistle gave them both, and when her eyes opened and she stretched out her arms to him, he was the happiest fairy in the world. The Brownies told her all that he had done, and how he had at last learned to be gentle, true, and brave.

"You shall have the crown, for you have worked so hard and you deserve it. I will have a wreath of flowers," said Lily, so glad and proud that she cared for nothing else.

"Keep your crown, for here are friends coming to bring Thistle his rewards," said the Brownies, and they pointed to a troop of earth spirits rising from among the mossy roots of an old tree. Sparkle brought a golden wand like the one he had earned for Lily. While she was giving it to Thistle, down through the air came the sky spirits, with the mantle of sunshine as their gift. Hardly had they folded it round happy Thistle when the sound of music, like drops falling in time and tune, was heard, and along the brook, in their boats of rosy shells, came the water sprites with a crown.

As they put it on his head, all took hands and danced about the two elves, shouting in their soft voices, "Thistledown and Lilybell! Long live our King and Queen!"

Little Bud

"Have you a tale for us too, dear Violeteye?" asked the Queen as Zephyr ceased. The little elf thus named looked from among the flower leaves where she sat and with a smile replied, "As I was weaving garlands in the field, I heard a primrose tell this tale to her friend Goldenrod. . . ."

"The naughty cuckoo has been here while we were gone and left this great blue egg among our little white ones," said the linnet to her mate as they came back from their breakfast one day and found the nest full.

"It is not a cuckoo's egg, my dear," answered the father bird, shaking his head. "Some fairy must have put it here; we must take care of it, or they may be angry and do harm to our little ones by and by. Sit carefully on it and see what will follow."

So Mama Linnet sat patiently on the five eggs for many days more, and then out came her four small children, who began to chirp for food. But the big blue egg still lay there, and no sound of a little bill pecking inside was heard.

"Shall we throw it out of the nest and make room for our babies?" asked the mother, finding her nursery very crowded.

"Not yet," said the careful papa, standing on one leg to rest, being very tired of bringing worms for his family. "Wait two more days, and then if the egg does not break, we will push it out."

He was a wise bird, and they were glad that they waited, for on the seventh day the blue egg suddenly flew open, and there lay the smallest, prettiest baby girl ever seen—three inches long, but rosy, gay, and lively as she popped up her curly head and looked about her much surprised to find herself in a nest swinging on the branch of a tree.

"Who are you?" asked the father linnet, and all the young ones stared at her with their big eyes and opened their beaks as if to eat her up.

"I'm little Bud," answered the tiny creature, smiling at them so sweetly that it was impossible to help loving her at once.

"Where do you come from?" said the mother.

"I don't know."

"Are you a fairy?"

"No, for I have no wand."

"A new kind of bird?"

"I have no feathers or wings."

"A human child?"

"I think not, for I have no parents."

"Bless the dear! What can she be? And what shall we do with her?" cried both the birds, much amazed at this new child of theirs.

Bud did not seem to be troubled at all, but lay rocking in her blue cradle and laughing at the young linnets who peeped curiously over the edge of it.

"She must have something to eat," said the papa, flying off.

"And some clothes," added the mama, bustling about.

But when a nice, fat worm was brought, Bud covered her face and cried with a shiver, "No, no! I cannot eat that ugly thing."

"Get a strawberry," said the mama, and she tried to wrap the largest, softest feather that lined her nest round the naked little maid.

But Bud kicked her small legs out of it at once and stood up, saying with a laugh, "I'm not a bird; I cannot wear feathers. Give me a pretty green leaf for a gown, and let me look about this big world where I find myself all at once."

So the linnet pulled a leaf and pecked two holes for Bud's arms and put it on her like a pinafore. She had never dressed a baby and did not know how, her own children being born with down coats that soon changed to gray feathers. But Bud looked very pretty in her green dress as she sat on the edge of the nest, staring about with her blue eyes and clapping her hands when the papa came flying home with a sweet wild berry in his bill for her breakfast. She ate it like an apple and drank a drop of dew that had fallen in the night; then she began to sing so sweetly that all the neighbors came to see what sort of bird Mrs. Linnet had hatched.

Much twittering and fluttering went on while they talked the matter over, asked many questions, and admired the pretty little creature who knew only her name and nothing more!

"Shall you keep her?" asked the robin, as he puffed out his red waistcoat and looked very wise.

"We dare not send her away," said the linnets.

"She will need a great deal of care," said the wren.

"You never can teach her to fly, and what will you do when your own children are gone?" asked the wood dove, who was very tenderhearted.

"You will have to make a new frock every day, and that will be so much work," said the yellow bird, who was very proud of her own gay gown and black velvet hood.

"I think some bad elf put her here to bring you trouble. I'd push her out of the nest and let her take care of herself," advised the woodpecker, wondering if the plump child would be as good to eat as the worm he hammered out of the trees.

"No, no!" cried the brown thrush. "She is too pretty to bring harm. Keep her till you see what she can do, and perhaps she may be a good sprite after all."

"She sings almost as well as I do, and I would like to add her songs to the many I already know," said the blackbird, who had lovely concerts in the meadow all by himself.

"Yes, we will wait a little, and if we cannot decide, by and by we will ask your advice, neighbors," said the linnets, beginning to feel rather proud of the curious stranger, since her coming made such a stir in the wood.

The birds flew away, and Bud settled down as one of the family, making herself so pleasant that all loved her and willingly crowded together to make room for her in the nest. The mother brooded over her at night and made her fresh gowns every day when the old ones withered up; the father brought her dew to wash in and to drink, and flew far and wide to find ripe berries for her to eat. The young birds, meanwhile, never tired of hearing her sing, watching her dance on the edge of the nest, or learning the pretty plays she taught them. Everyone was very kind and waited patiently to see what would come. But when at last the little birds flew away, the parents wanted to go with them, but they did not like to leave Bud all alone.

"I'm not afraid," she said, "for now I am strong enough to take care of myself. All the birds know me, and I shall not be lonely. Carry me down to the grass below and let me run about and find my own food and clothes as your children do. I won't forget you, but you need not trouble about me anymore."

So Papa Linnet took her on his back, as often before, and flew down to the softest place below, and there they left her with a tender goodbye; for they had to watch over their young ones, who were trying their wings and wandering far and wide.

"I shall be taken care of as the flowers are," said Bud when she found herself sitting on a pebble beside the path that went through the pleasant wood full of happy little creatures busy with their work or play.

"I wish I were a bird, for then I could fly about and see the world; or a fairy, for then I could do splendid things; or even a flower for someone to love and carry away. I wonder what I was made for and what I can do—such a little thing in this great world! I'm sure I don't know, but I can be happy and kind and try to help all I see. Then I shall make friends and not feel lonely very long."

As she said this, brave Bud looked about her to see whom she could help first, and she spied an ant tugging a large white bundle along. It looked as if he were taking clothes to some fairy washerwoman, but in fact the bundle was an egg, and the ant-nurse was bringing it up from the nest to lie awhile in the warm sun to grow.

He told Bud all about it when she offered to help, and very gladly let her watch this egg while he and the other nurses went down for many more. Soon they lay all about in a quiet corner, where the sun shone on them, and Bud went to and fro, turning them and keeping guard over them lest some hungry bird should snap them up.

"Now I'm useful," she said, quite happy in her new work, though she was only a nursery maid and had no wages but the thanks of the busy ants. By and by the eggs were carried down, and she was free to go on her travels again. The grass was like a forest to her, the mounds of moss were high hills, a little brook a great river, and a patch of sand a desert to be crossed.

"First I will dress myself nicely," said Bud, and coming to a wild rosebush, she gathered up several of the fallen leaves and tried to fasten them together with the thorns. But her little hands could not manage the pretty pink skirt, and the thorns pricked her tender flesh as she folded the leaves over her bosom. She was about to give up in despair and put on the faded green one again when a wood spider, who sat in his hole near by, said kindly, "Come here, little lady! I can spin and weave, and I'll sew your dress for you with pleasure. I saw you helping my neighbors the ants so I will help you."

Bud was very glad of this kind offer and watched the spider at this work as he sewed the pink leaves together with his silver thread as neatly as a seamstress, putting a line of embroidery all round the hem and twisting a silken cord to tie it at the waist.

"Oh, how pretty you are!" cried the spider when the dress was on. "You must have a veil to keep the sun out of your eyes. Here is my last web," and he threw the shining gauze over her head, making her look like a little bride under the silvery veil.

Bud thanked him very much and went happily on, till she came to a party of columbines dancing in the wind. They thought she was the spirit of a rose come to visit them and lowered their scarlet horns to offer her the honey in the tower ends.

She was just wondering where she should find some dinner, and here was a delicious feast all ready for her, thanks to the pretty dress that made the columbines think her a flower. She threw up her veil and told them her story, which they thought very interesting and rather sad.

"Stay and live with us, little darling!" they cried. "You are too delicate to go about all alone. The wind will blow you away, some foot will crush you, or some cruel wasp kill you with its sting. Live here, and we will be your friends and feed and care for you."

"You are very kind, and your home is very pleasant, but I must go on. I feel sure that I have something to do, that somewhere I shall find my place and sometime have a pair of wings, to be either a bird or a fairy," answered Bud as she rested by the rock round which the flowers grew.

"Here comes our good friend Honey-bag, the bee. He is very wise; perhaps he can tell you where you should go and what you are," said the columbines. They nodded joyfully as the brown velvet bee came buzzing along, for he was their postman and brought the daily news.

Eagerly they told him all about their little guest and asked him if he had heard anything of a featherless bird, a strayed elf, or a human changeling hidden in a blue egg.

The bee said he once heard a hummingbird tell about some little creatures who were neither children nor fairies, but instead were made out of the fancies in people's heads. These poor mites never could be real boys and girls, but if they tried very hard, and were very good, wings would grow and they would be elves at last.

"I will, I will!" cried Bud. "I know I'm one of those creatures, and I want to be a fairy and find my home by and by. How shall I do it?"

"I think you have begun very well, for I've heard of you from several friends as I came through the wood, and all say good words of you. Go on, and I am sure you will find your wings at last. I will do my part and give you something to eat as you travel along."

As the kind bee spoke, he began to mix the yellow pollen and honey he had gathered, and soon handed Bud a nice little loaf of bee-bread to carry with her. She folded it up in a sweet-scented napkin of white violet leaves, and with a horn of honey from the columbines, set out again with many thanks and full of hope and courage.

Presently a cloud of gay butterflies came flocking round her, crying out, "Here's a rose! I smell honey! Come and taste! No, it is an elf! Dance with us, little dear!"

Bud admired them very much and felt very glad and proud when they alighted all over her; she looked like one great butterfly with wings of every color.

"I cannot play with you because I am not an elf, but if you will carry me on my way toward Fairyland, I will give you my honey and my bread, for I go very slowly and want to get along as quickly as I can," said Bud, thinking that these pretty insects might help her.

The butterflies were idle things and hated to work, but they wanted the dainty loaf and the flower sweets, so they said they would try to carry Bud and save her tired little feet. They held tightly to her belt, her hair, her frock, and all flew up at once, lifting her a little way above the ground and carrying her along in a cloud of blue, yellow, red, and brown wings, fluttering as they went. It was hard work, and soon the smaller ones let go.

Bud began to fall, and they were forced to lay her down on the grass while they rested and ate every crumb of the bee-bread.

"Take me a little farther and then you shall have the honey," said wise Bud, who was anxious to get on and saw that the lazy butterflies would leave her as soon as her provisions were gone.

"Up again!" cried the great black and golden one, and away they went, all tugging stoutly. But though the tiny maid was as light as a feather, they had little strength in either legs or wings, and soon dropped her with a bump in the dusty path below.

"Thanks! Here's the horn. Now let me rest and get over my fall," said Bud, making up her mind that her own feet were safest, after all.

The butterflies flew away, and the small traveler sat up to see where she was. A dismal groaning caught her ear, and close by she saw a rusty old beetle feebly trying to dig a hole in the sand.

"What is the matter?" asked Bud.

"It is time to die and I want to bury myself, but I'm so weak that I'm afraid I shall not get my grave ready in time, and then I shall be eaten up by some bird or crushed by some giant's foot," answered the beetle, kicking and shoveling away as hard as he could.

"But if you were dead, you would not know it," said Bud.

"Stupid child! If I'm killed in that way, I cannot live again; but if I bury myself and lie asleep till spring, I come up a grub or a young beetle. So I want a good grave to rest in; for dying is only a sleep before we wake up in another shape."

"I'm glad of that!" cried Bud. "I'll help you dig and I'll cover you nicely and hope that you will be some pretty insect by and by."

So she threw off her veil and worked busily with a little wooden shovel till a deep grave was made. The old beetle tumbled in with a gruff "Thank you, child," and died quite comfortably with the warm sand over him. Bud piled little stones above the place and left him to his long sleep, happy to be able to help and full of wonder as to whether she, too, would have to die before her change came.

The sun was going down now, for the butterfly party and the beetle's funeral had taken a long time.

"I must find a place to sleep," said Bud rather anxiously. This was her first night alone, and she began to miss Mama Linnet's warm wings brooding over her.

But she kept up her courage and trudged on till she was so tired that she was forced to stop and rest on a bank where a glowworm had just lighted its little lamp.

"Can I stay here under this big leaf?" she asked, glad to see the friendly light and to bathe her tired feet in the dewy grass.

"You cannot go much farther, for the marsh is close by, and I see you have no wings, so you never could get across," answered the worm, turning his green lamp full upon the weary little wanderer.

Bud told her story and was just going to ask if there was anything to eat— for she was sadly hungry—when some very sweet voices called down to her from a tall bush over her head, "Come to us, dear! We are the marsh honeysuckles, cousins of the columbines you met today. Here is supper, with a bed and a warm welcome for the good little creature Honey-bag the bee told us about."

Bud put up her arms to a great cluster of white flowers bending down to her, and in a moment lay in a delicious place full of the sweetest fragrance. The honeysuckles fed and petted and rocked her to sleep before she could half thank them for their kindness.

There was time for a good nap and a lovely dream before a harsh voice awoke her, and she heard a bat talking as it hung near by, its leathery wings closed over its eyes to shut out the light of the glowworm, who was still strolling about on the bank.

"Yes, the poor little boy wandered into the bog and was nearly drowned," said the bat. "It was naughty Willy Wisp playing tricks again and leading people from the right path to splash into the mud. I've scolded him many a time, but he continues to do it, for he loves to make the woodsmen and the children think he is the light in their cottage windows, so that they stray from the path and fall into the marsh."

"What a wicked fellow!" cried Bud, rubbing her eyes and sitting up to listen.

"Of course, he wouldn't mind you, for he knows you hate light, and he likes to tease you by flashing his lantern in your eyes," said the glowworm to the bat.

"Yes, I do hate light of all kinds, and wish it were always night," scolded the bat.

"I don't!" said Bud. "I love sunshine and stars and glowworms and all the bright things. Perhaps if I went and talked to Willy Wisp he would stop playing these naughty pranks," she continued, feeling that this would be a very good deed to do for the dear children.

"You couldn't keep him out of mischief unless you told stories all night. He loves tales dearly, but he won't stay still and listen unless they are always new and *very* charming," said the bat, peeping out with one eye to see who the stranger might be.

"I know hundreds, for I was born of a fancy, and my head is full of lovely ones. And I sing such merry songs that all the birds used to listen to me for hours. If I could only reach this Willy Wisp, I think I could amuse him till the people got safely home," said Bud.

"Come and try; I'll carry you," said the bat, shutting his wings and looking like a black mouse as he crept nearer for Bud to mount.

"No, no, stay with us, and don't go to that dismal marsh full of ugly things and bad air," cried the honeysuckles, trying to hold her fast with soft, sticky hands.

But Bud was eager to do all the good she might, and bravely mounted her new horse, singing as she flew away,

> *On the bat's back I do fly*
> *After summer, merrily.*

"She won't succeed," said the glowworm, putting out his lamp as he went to bed.

"Alas, no! Poor little thing! She will die over there and never be a fairy," sighed the flowers, looking like sad white ghosts in the dim light.

A cloud of fireflies danced over the marsh; frogs croaked, mosquitoes hummed, and tall yellow lilies rang their freckled bells. The air was damp and hot. A white mist rose from the water that glimmered between the forests of reeds and the islands of bog moss, and sleek muskrats and bright-eyed snakes glided about, while wild ducks slept with their heads under their wings in quiet corners.

It was a strange, shadowy place, and Bud's heart died within her as she thought of staying there alone. But she did want to see if she could make the bad Willy behave better and not lead poor people into danger, so she held fast while the bat skimmed to and fro looking for the naughty fellow. Soon he came dancing toward them, a dark little body with a big head like a round lantern, all shining with the light inside.

"What have you brought me, old Leather-wing? A pretty bride to cheer up the marsh or an elf to dance at my ball tonight?" he said, looking at Bud with delight as she sat on the dusky bat, her pink dress and silvery veil glimmering in the brightness that now shone over her like moonlight.

"No, it is a famous storyteller, come to amuse you when you are tired of whisking about and doing mischief. Be very polite or I will take her away again," answered the bat, setting Bud down on a small green island among the bulrushes and tall marsh moss.

"Let us hear one. Stop croaking, Speckle-back, and do you ladies quit dancing while I listen. Go along, Leather-wing. She shall stay till tomorrow and see what she can do," said Willy Wisp, seating himself near Bud. The frogs grew still and the fireflies settled on the leaves like little lamps, making the island as light as day.

"It is late now, so when you hear the clock strike twelve, you can stop and go to sleep, for the people will all be safe at home and Willy can do no harm. I'll come again soon. Goodnight."

And away skimmed the bat, glad to find the darkest part of the marsh and hunt gnats for supper.

Bud immediately began to tell the story of "The Merry Cockchafer," and it proved so very interesting that soon a circle of frogs surrounded the island, laughing with their great mouths and winking their bright eyes as they listened. The wild ducks woke up and came to hear, and a watersnake glided nearer, with his neighbor the muskrat. The fireflies grew so thick on the reeds and moss that everything sparkled, and Willy Wisp nodded his bright head joyfully as he sat like a king with his court about him.

Just when the story became most exciting, when the Cockchafer and the Stag-beetle were going to fight a duel over the lovely white moth, the clock struck twelve, and Bud, who was very tired, stopped short, saying, "I will finish tomorrow at twilight. The last part is the best, for the Ladybug and the wicked Grasshopper do terrible things in it."

They all begged eagerly for the end, but Bud was hoarse and had to go to sleep. So everyone went away to talk about this new and charming creature who had come to make the long nights pleasant. Willy Wisp went zigzagging to and fro, trying to imagine what would come next, and Bud laid her head on a bulrush pillow to dream of stars till morning.

She was rather troubled, when daylight came, to find herself a prisoner, for deep water was all round her island, and there was no way of escaping. She asked a pretty white duck to take her to a larger place, for here there was nothing to eat but the soft green buds of the sweet flag and the little sour balls of the wild cranberry vines.

"I'm not a steamer, and I don't carry passengers," answered the duck, paddling away, for he wanted Bud to stay and tell more tales.

So there she had to live for many days, watching the long-legged herons as they stalked about fishing in the pools, seeing how the rats built their curious houses, how the frogs leaped and dived, how the snakes glided to and fro, and how the

GENIAL & FAMILIAR
CONVERSE WITH
&ALSO THE
LEOPARD
FROG

THOREAU

ducklings ate flies all day long. She talked with the yellow lilies, learned the song of the whispering reeds, and climbed up the tall stems of the bulrushes to look out over the marsh, longing to be on firm ground again. The bat forgot to come and see her, and Willy grew so fond of her stories that he would sit for hours while she told them. No one came to harm, and Bud felt that she was really doing a good thing all alone out there on the dreary bog. Everyone loved her and wanted her to stay, but by and by the summer was over, the fireflies died, and Willy Wisp grew pale and lazy and fell asleep easier each night, as if he, too, were ready to fade away till hot weather should make him lively and bright again.

"Now I might go if I could find any friend to help me," said Bud when the wild ducks said goodbye and the herons stalked away.

"I will help you," said a watersnake, popping his head up with a kinder look than one would fancy such fiery eyes could wear.

"You!" said Bud, much surprised, for she had never liked the snake very much, though she had always been kind to him.

"I am your friend if you will have me. No one cares for me. I am so ugly and have had a bad name ever since the world began, but I hope when I shed my skin I may be handsomer or change to something better. So I try to be a good snake and do what I can to make my neighbors happy."

"Poor thing! I hope you will be a pretty green adder and live among the flowers like one I once knew. It must be hard to be contented here, and you are very kind to want to help me," said Bud, laying her little warm hand on the ugly head of the snake, who had crept up to bask in the sun.

That pleased the snake very much, for no one ever petted him, and his eyes shone like jewels as he coiled his slender body nearer Bud's feet and lifted up his head to answer her.

"You want to go away and you shall. We shall all miss you sadly, but it will soon be cold, and you need stay no longer. I will ask my friend Sleek the muskrat to gnaw these strong rushes till they fall and make bridges across the pools. You can go safely over them and find some warm, pretty place to live till the summer comes again."

"That is a fine plan! Thank you, dear friend. Let us do it at once while Willy is asleep and no one sees us," cried Bud.

So Sleek the muskrat came and made a road for her from one tuft of grass to another, till she was safely on the land. Then she bade these ugly but kind friends goodbye and gladly ran about the pleasant field where autumn flowers were going to seed and dead leaves falling fast. She feasted on wild grapes, fried berries, and apples fallen from the trees since the harvest was carried in. Everything was getting ready for winter, and Bud was glad to make herself a warm suit of mullein clothes, and a little hood of thistledown. She was fitting beechnut shells on her tiny feet when a withered plant nearby called out to her, "Are you going far, that you put on new clothes and stout boots, little stranger?"

"I must travel till I find my own country, no matter how far away it is. Can I do any errand for you?" asked Bud kindly.

"Yes. Will you carry these seeds of mine to the great meadow over there? All my friends are there, and I long to be at home again. Someone picked me last spring and dropped me here, but I did not die. I took root and bloomed here, and must always stay unless someone will take my seeds back. Then I shall come up in my own place next spring and be a happy flower again."

"I will do it," said Bud, "but I thought the wind took your seeds about for you."

"Some are too heavy. Pine seeds, maple keys, thistle, and dandelion down blow about, but some of us grow from our roots, and some, like me, come from seeds kept in little bags. I'm called Shepherd's purse, and I'm a humble weed, but I love my own people and long to see them again."

"You shall!" cried Bud, and gathering the three-cornered bags, she took them carefully away to the meadow, where other plants like this one were glad to hear of their lost friend and to watch over the gift she sent them.

Remembering how pleasant and comfortable it was to find various flowers blooming along the roadside like hospitable inns for tiny travelers like herself, good Bud spent several days planting roots and seeds beside the path that led through the meadow.

"Now children, birds, butterflies, and fairies will be glad to find these pretty things blooming here, though they will never know who planted them," she said when the last task was done.

The frost had come, and nuts were rattling down, leaves turning brown, and cold winds beginning to blow. So poor Bud looked about as she went through the woods, hoping to find some safe, warm place to sleep, because she felt sure that when the snow came she would die, so small and delicate and friendless was the dear little thing. When she came to a great oak, she sat down on an acorn cup and tried to break the hard shell of an acorn that she might nibble a bit for her dinner. She could not do it and was sitting wondering sadly what would become of her when a sweet acorn without its shell dropped into her lap. Looking up, she saw a gray squirrel peeping at her from a branch above her head. She smiled and thanked him, and he came down to sit opposite and look at her with his fine tail over his head like an umbrella.

"I know you, little maid, and I'm glad you came here, for I can show you a charming house for the winter. I heard you tell a field mouse how lonely you were, and I saw tears dropping just now as you sat here thinking you had not a friend in the world," said the squirrel, whose name was Dart, as he nodded at her and kindly cracked a chestnut to follow the acorn if she needed more.

"Everyone is very kind to me, but everyone seems to go to sleep when autumn comes. So I felt alone and sad and expected to die in the snow. But if I can find a cozy place to live until spring, I shall be very glad and will do anything I can to pay for it," answered Bud, much comforted by her good dinner and a kind word.

"If you will help me get in my nuts and acorns and moss and leaves for winter food and bedding, I will let you use the Kobolds' house till they come. They are jolly little fellows, and they will allow you to stay and teach you to spin, for they spin all winter and make lovely cloth for the elves out of silkweed and thistledown. Here is their house. I hide it and take care of it while they are gone and get it ready for them in the autumn, as they come with the first snow."

While Dart spoke, he had been clearing away a pile of dead leaves at the foot of the old oak, and soon Bud saw an arched doorway leading into the hollow trunk, where the roots made different chambers and all was dry and warm and cozy as a little house. She went in and looked about, well pleased at what she saw and very glad for such a comfortable home. She hoped the Kobolds would let her ſtay, and set to work at once to help Dart get ready for them. The sky looked dark with snow, and a cold wind ruſtled through the wood.

In one room they ſtored nuts and acorns, rose, holly berries, a dried apple or two, and many pinecones to burn. Dart showed her a fireplace, and told her the Kobolds kept themselves very warm and jolly at their work. In another room, they ſpread moss and dry grass for beds, and there the seven Kobolds would sleep like door mice. The empty cocoon of a caterpillar ſtill hung in one corner, and Bud said that should be her hammock, with a curtain made of woven yellow bindweed hung before the nook. They swept the floor with fir-needle brooms and ſpread a carpet of red oak leaves, which gave a gay air to the place. Then Dart left Bud to fill a row of acorn cups with water from a ſpring near by, and he ran off to nibble ſplinters from the pîtch pines to make torches for the Kobolds, who worked in the evening and needed light.

Bud was as happy as a girl with a new dollhouse, and she looked like a tiny doll herself as she buſtled to and fro, filling her tubs, duſting her pretty rooms, and getting ready for the seven ſtrangers, like Snow Whîte. All was ready in two days, and Dart had time to lay in his own ſtores before the snow came. Bud watched over the heaps of nuts he piled, leſt Dart's sly neighbors ſteal them while he ran up and down, tucking them away in holes about the oak tree. This helped him much, and he was very fond of her, and together they got up a nice surprise for the Kobolds by putting in new beds for them made of cheſtnut burrs, which rocked on their outside prickles like cradles and were lined with down as soft as silk.

"That will tickle them," said Dart, "and when they know that you thought of it, they will like you as much as I do. Now rest a bit, and be ready to welcome them, for I'm sure they will come today. I'll run to the treetop and look out for them, and you can light the fire when I give the word."

Dart whisked away, and Bud stood in the doorway with a warm mat of hemlock sprigs under her feet and a garland of evergreen overhead. She had trimmed the arch and stuck bits of gay holly all about to welcome the little men. Soon snowflakes began to flutter down, and Bud rejoiced that she had a nice, warm house to stay in instead of freezing to death like a lost bird. Suddenly Dart called from the treetop, "They are coming!" and hurried down to rub two sticks together till a spark flew out and set the pinecone on the hearth ablaze. "Run to the door when you see them," he said, fanning the fire with his bushy tail in a great state of excitement.

Bud peeped out and was just going to say "I see nothing but snow" when she saw that what looked like a party of flakes blowing up to the door was really the seven Kobolds, loaded with great piles of white silkweed for their spinning. She dropped her best curtsy, smiled her sweetest smile, and called out, "Welcome home, my masters!" like a little maid servant, and she led the way to the large room, now bright and warm with the fire roaring up the chimney made by a hole in the old roots.

"Ha, ha! Neighbor Dart, you have done well this time, and we are satisfied with you. Now just store away our packs while we go for our wheels, and then we will have supper. But first, tell us who this pretty person is, if you please?" said the oldest of the

Kobolds, and the others stood nodding and looking at Bud as if she pleased them well.

"Your new housekeeper, gentlemen," answered Dart, and in a few words told them about this friend, how she had helped get ready for them, what fine tales and songs she knew, and how much good she had done and still hoped to do while waiting for her wings to grow.

"Good, very good! She shall stay with us, and we will take care of her till spring. Then we will see what happens." And they all smiled and nodded harder than ever, as if they knew something charming but would not tell it yet.

Then they trotted away before Bud could thank them half enough. While they were gone, Dart showed her how to put a row of chestnuts on the hearth to roast, and how to set the table, which was a dry mushroom propped up on four legs in the middle of the room, with toadstools to sit on. Acorn cups full of berries and water and grains of wheat and barley were arranged on it, with a place for the chestnuts when they were done, and some preserved apple on an oak-leaf platter. Several torches were lighted and stuck in holes at the four corners of the table, and then all was ready. Bud put on a white apron made of her torn veil and waited like a neat cook to dish up supper when her masters arrived.

Presently they came, each lugging a tiny spinning wheel on his back from the cave among the rocks where they hid them during the summer. Dart helped them settle down and then left them to eat and rest, and Bud waited on them so nicely that they wondered how they ever got on without a maid before. She was not at all afraid of them now, for they were jolly little fellows with fat bodies, thin legs, rosy faces, and sharp eyes. All were dressed in white down suits and wore droll pointed hats made of some seed pod and boots of magic stuff that carried them great distances, as if blown by the wind.

They liked their supper very much, and ate and drank and chatted pleasantly till all were done. Then they sat round the fire and smoked sweet fern in Indian pipes till Bud had cleared away.

"Now come and sing to us," they said, and the youngest Kobold politely set a stool in the warmest corner for her.

So Bud sang all her gayest songs, to their great delight, and told her adventures till it was time to sleep. The little men were charmed with their new beds, and pulling poppy-pod nightcaps over their heads, tumbled in with drowsy goodnights, leaving Bud to cover up the fire, shut the front door, and put out the lights. Soon she was in her own soft hammock; and nothing broke the silence but the sigh of the wind, the tap of falling snowflakes on dry leaves outside, and seven little snores as the tired Kobolds dreamed cozily in their new beds.

Bud was up early the next day, and had everything ready when the little men came out to breakfast. Afterward they set their wheels whirling, and all day long they spun busily till many skeins of shining silk were ready to be woven into elfin cloth. Bud soon learned to spin, too, and they made her a wheel so she could work with them. They seldom spoke, and never ate or stopped till night. Then the wheels stood still and the spinners went out for a run while Bud got supper.

In the evening, if there was moonlight, they had gay times in the wood, whisking Bud with them, and sliding down hillocks of snow on their sleds of bark while Dart looked on, well wrapped up in his gray fur coat.

But stormy nights they sat at home and told stories or played games, and they were very merry, teaching Bud many wise and interesting things. The Kobolds knew all kinds of fairies, nixies, goblins, and spirits, and had been in many lands.

It was very pleasant, but when the last month of winter came, Bud began to be so sleepy that she could not keep her eyes open, and sat nodding as she spun, gaping instead of singing, and was often found dreaming in her bed when she should have been at work. She was much troubled about it, but the Kobolds only laughed, slyly feeling of her shoulders and telling her to sleep away, for their work was nearly done and they did not need her.

One morning, Bud did not wake up at all, and when the little men peeped at her, there she lay rolled up in her hammock, very like a chrysalis in its shell.

"All right," laughed the imps, nodding to one another, "let her sleep while the wings grow, and in May she will wake up to a prettier surprise than the one she gave us."

So they finished their work and packed up the silk, and as soon as the snow was gone, they hid their wheels, had a farewell feast with Dart, and departed, begging him to watch over Bud and have their house ready for them next year.

Day after day the grass grew greener, the buds larger, the air warmer, and the world more beautiful, but still Bud lay asleep in her little bed, where the faithful squirrel went every morning to see that she was safe. May came at last, and the pink flowers under the leaves pushed out their rosy faces. Birds sang among the green bushes, and the sun shone brightly as the little wood creatures ventured out one by one for another happy summer.

Then Bud woke from her long sleep, stretched her small arms and legs like a baby after its nap, looked about her to see where she was, and sprang up, fearing it was too late to get the Kobolds' breakfast. But the house was empty, the fire was out, the wheels gone, and there was nothing to be seen but a lovely white silk dress lying on the table, with her name woven in tiny buds all over it. While she was looking at it with delight, Dart came in and skipped for joy to see her awake again and prettier than ever, for while she slept she had grown very beautiful. Her winter gown was withered up and fell off as she got out of bed, leaving her all ready for the new white gown, which she gladly put on.

"Pull away my old hood that lies there on my shoulders and let me tie my pretty dress with this fine belt," said Bud, feeling something on her back.

Dart's black eyes sparkled as he answered with a gay whisk, "Shake yourself and see what happens. But don't go till I have time to admire the splendid princess ready for Fairyland."

Bud shook, and, lo, a pair of blue and silver wings unfolded from her little shoulders. There she stood, a shining creature, gay as a butterfly, delicate as an elf, lovely as a happy child, and Dart waved his tail like a banner and cried joyfully, "The Kobolds said it would be so, because you tried so hard to be and do good! Now you can go home and lead a happy life in Fairyland."

Bud could only clap her hands and laugh for joy and try to see the beautiful wings she had worked and waited for so long.

"Thank you very much for all your kindness to me, dear Dart. I will come again and see you and the little men if I can. Now I must go and try to fly before I set out for home," she said, and hastened to the door, where wood violets were watching for her with eager blue eyes, and the robins, wrens, and linnets sang to welcome her.

There was no need to learn how to fly; the lovely wings lifted her lightly up, and away she went like a newborn butterfly, glittering in the sunshine. It was so delightful that she could hardly bear to come down to the earth again, so she perched on a high branch of the old oak and took a peep at Dart's home before she said goodbye to him.

"How shall I find my way to Fairyland?" she asked, eager to be off, for the longing was stronger than ever in her heart.

"I have come to show you the road," answered a small shrill voice, and a splendid hummingbird alighted on the branch beside her, its breast sparkling like a jewel, its long bill full of honey, and its quivering wings making the softest music.

"I am ready! Goodbye, dear friends! Goodbye, great world! I love you, but I must go to my own people," cried Bud. And with a flash of the blue and silver wings, she was gone.

But for many a winter's night, her story was told by the Kobolds as they spun around the fire. And for many a long day did bird, bee, beetle, ant, and flower love and remember little Bud.

The Fairy Flower

"Now, little Sunbeam, what have you to tell us?" said the Queen, looking down on a bright-eyed elf, who was half hidden in the deep moss. "Something I heard a harebell tell," replied the fairy, and in a low, sweet voice she began to tell the tale. . . .

In a large and pleasant garden sat little Annie all alone. She seemed very sad, for drops that were not dew fell fast upon the flowers beside her, who looked wonderingly up and bent nearer, as if they longed to cheer and comfort her. The warm wind lifted up her shining hair and softly kissed her cheek, while the sunbeams, looking most kindly in her face, made little rainbows in her tears and lingered lovingly about her. But Annie paid no heed to sun, or wind, or flower; still the bright tears fell, and she forgot all but her sorrow.

"Little Annie, tell me why you weep," said a low voice in her ear, and looking up, the child beheld a little figure standing on a vine at her side. A lovely face smiled on her from amid bright locks of hair, and shining wings were folded on a white and glittering robe that fluttered in the wind.

"Who are you, lovely little thing?" cried Annie, smiling through her tears.

"I am a fairy, little child, and have come to help and comfort you," replied the spirit. "Now tell me why you weep, and let me be your friend," and she smiled more kindly still on Annie's wondering face.

"Are you really a little elf, such as I read of in my fairy books? Do you ride on butterflies, sleep in flower cups, and live among the clouds?"

"Yes, all these things I do, and many stranger still that all your fairy books can never tell. But now, dear Annie," said the fairy, bending nearer, "tell me why I found no sunshine on your face. Why are these great drops shining on the flowers, and why do you sit alone when bird and bee are calling you to play?"

"Ah, you will not love me anymore if I should tell you all," said Annie, while the tears began to fall again. "I am not happy, for I am not good. How shall I learn to be a patient, gentle child? Good little fairy, will you teach me how?"

"Gladly will I aid you, Annie. But if you truly wish to be a happy child, you first must learn to conquer many passions that you cherish now, and make your heart a home for gentle feelings and happy thoughts. The task is hard, but I will give this fairy flower to help and counsel you. Bend hither so that I may place it on your breast. No hand can take it hence till I unsay the spell that holds it there."

And as thus she spoke, the elf took from her bosom a graceful flower whose snow-white leaves shone with a strange, soft light. "This is a fairy flower," said the elf, "invisible to every eye save yours. Now listen while I tell its power, Annie: when your heart is filled with loving thoughts, when some kindly deed has been done, some duty well performed, then from the flower there will arise the sweetest, softest fragrance to reward and gladden you. But when an unkind word is on your lips, when a selfish, angry feeling rises in your heart or an unkind, cruel deed is to be done, then will you hear the soft, low chime of the flower bell. Listen to its warning; let the word remain unspoken, the deed undone, and in the quiet joy of your own heart and the magic perfume of your bosom flower, you will find a sweet reward."

"Oh kind and generous fairy, how can I ever thank you for this lovely gift!" cried Annie. "I will be true and listen to my little bell whenever it may ring. But shall I never see you more? Ah! If you would only stay with me, I should indeed be good."

"I cannot stay now, little Annie," said the elf, "but when another spring comes round, I shall be here again, to see how well the fairy gift has done its work. And now farewell; be faithful to yourself, and the magic flower will never fade."

Then the gentle fairy folded her little arms around Annie's neck, laid a soft kiss on her cheek, and spreading wide her shining wings, flew singing up among the white clouds floating in the sky.

And little Annie sat among her flowers and watched with wondering joy the fairy blossom shining on her breast.

The pleasant days of spring and summer passed away, and in little Annie's garden autumn flowers were blooming everywhere, with each day's sun and dew growing still more beautiful and bright. But the fairy flower, which should have been the loveliest of all, hung pale and drooping on Annie's bosom. Its fragrance seemed quite gone, and the clear, low music of its warning chime rang often in her ear.

When first the fairy placed it there, Annie had been pleased with her new gift and for a while obeyed the bell. She also tried to win some fragrance from the flower by kind and pleasant words and actions finding, as the fairy had said, a sweet reward in the strange, soft perfume of the magic blossom, shining upon her breast. But selfish thoughts would come to tempt her, she would yield, and unkind words would fall from her lips. Then the flower drooped pale and scentless, the bell rang mournfully, and Annie forgot her better resolutions and became again a selfish, willful little child.

At last she tried no longer, but grew angry with the faithful flower and would have torn it from her breast if she could. But the fairy spell held it fast, and all her angry words only made it ring a louder, sadder peal. Each day she grew still more unhappy, discontented, and unkind. She was no better for the gentle fairy's gift, and longed for spring, that it might be returned. For now the constant echo of the mournful music made her very sad.

One sunny morning, when the fresh, cool winds were blowing and not a cloud was in the sky, little Annie walked among her flowers, looking carefully into each, hoping thus to find the fairy, who alone could take the magic blossom from her breast. But she lifted up their drooping leaves and peeped into their dewy cups in vain; no little elf lay hidden there, and she turned sadly from them all, saying, "I will go out into the fields and woods, and seek her there. I will not listen to this tiresome music more, nor wear this withered flower longer." So out into the fields she went, where the long grass rustled as she passed and timid birds looked at her from their nests; where lovely wildflowers nodded in the wind and opened wide their fragrant leaves to welcome in the murmuring bees; where butterflies like winged flowers danced and glittered in the sun.

Little Annie looked, searched, and asked them all if anyone could tell her of the fairy whom she sought. But the birds looked wonderingly at her with their soft, bright eyes, and still sang on; the flowers nodded wisely on their stems, but did not speak; the butterfly and bee buzzed and fluttered away, one far too busy, the other too idle, to stay and tell her what she asked.

Then she went through broad fields of yellow grain that waved around her like a golden forest. Here crickets chirped, grasshoppers leaped, and busy ants worked, but they could not tell her what she longed to know.

"Now will I go among the hills," said Annie. "She may be there." So up and down the green hillsides went her little feet; long she searched and vainly she called, but still no fairy came. Then by the riverside she went and asked the gay dragonflies and the cool white lilies if the fairy had been there. But the blue waves rippled on the white sand at her feet, and no voice answered her.

Then into the forest little Annie went, and as she passed along the dim, cool paths, the wood flowers smiled up in her face, gay squirrels peeped at her as they swung amid the vines, and doves cooed softly as she wandered by. But none could answer her. Weary with her long and useless search, she sat amid the ferns and feasted on the rosy strawberries that grew beside her, watching meanwhile the crimson evening clouds that glowed around the setting sun.

The night wind rustled through the boughs, rocking the flowers to sleep; the wild birds sang their evening hymns, and all within the wood grew calm and still. Paler and paler grew the purple light, lower and lower drooped little Annie's head. The tall ferns bent to shield her from the dew, the whispering pines sang a soft lullaby, and when the autumn moon rose, her silver light shone on the child, now pillowed on green moss, asleep amid the flowers in the dim old forest.

And all night long beside her stood the fairy she had sought, and by elfin spell and charm sent to the sleeping child this dream.

Little Annie dreamed she sat in her own garden, as she had often sat before, with angry feelings in her heart and unkind words upon her lips. The magic flower was ringing its soft warning, but she paid no heed to anything, save her own troubled thoughts. Thus she sat, when suddenly a low voice whispered in her ear, "Little Annie, look and see the evil things that you are cherishing. I will clothe in fitting shapes the thoughts and feelings that now dwell within your heart, and you shall see how great their power becomes, if you don't banish them forever."

Then Annie saw, with fear and wonder, that the angry words she uttered changed to dark, unlovely forms, each showing plainly from what fault or passion it had sprung. Some of the shapes had scowling faces and bright, fiery eyes: these were the spirits of anger. Others, with sullen, anxious looks, seemed gathering up all they could reach, and Annie saw that the more they gained, the less they seemed to have. These she knew were shapes of selfishness. Spirits of pride folded their shadowy garments round them and turned scornfully away from all the rest. These

and many others Annie saw, which had come from her own heart and taken form before her eyes.

When first she saw them, they were small and weak; but as she looked, they seemed to grow and gather strength, and each gained a strange power over her. She could not drive them from her sight, and they seemed to cast black shadows all around, dimming the sunshine, blighting the flowers, and driving away all bright and lovely things. Rising slowly round her, Annie saw a high, dark wall that seemed to shut out everything she loved; she dared not move or speak, but with a strange fear in her heart sat watching the dim hovering shapes.

Higher and higher rose the shadowy wall; slowly the flowers near her died and lingeringly the sunlight faded, until they both were gone and she was left all alone behind the gloomy wall. Then the spirits gathered round her, whispering strange things in her ear, bidding her obey, for by her own will she had yielded up her heart to be their home, and she was now their slave. She could hear no more, and sinking down among the withered flowers, she wept sad and bitter tears for her lost liberty and joy. Then through the gloom there shone a faint, soft light, and on her breast she saw her fairy flower, upon whose snow-white leaves her tears lay shining.

Clearer and brighter grew the radiant light, till the evil spirits turned away to the dark shadow of the wall and left the child alone.

The light and perfume of the flower seemed to bring new strength to Annie, and she rose up, saying, as she bent to kiss the blossom on her breast, "Dear flower, help and guide me now, and I will listen to your voice and cheerfully obey my faithful fairy bell."

Then in her dream she felt how hard the spirits tried to tempt and trouble her, and how, but for her flower, they would have led her back and made all dark and dreary as before. Long and hard she struggled, and tears often fell; but after each new trial, brighter shone her magic flower and sweeter grew its breath, while the spirits lost still more their power to tempt her. Meanwhile, green flowering vines crept up the high, dark wall, and soon, wherever green leaves and flowers bloomed, the evil spirits fled away. In their place came shining forms with gentle eyes and smiling lips, who gathered round her with such loving words, and brought such strength and joy to Annie's heart, that nothing evil dared to enter in. Slowly sank the gloomy wall, and, over wreaths of fragrant flowers, Annie passed out into the pleasant world again, the fairy gift no longer pale and drooping but now shining like a star upon her breast.

Then the low voice spoke again in Annie's sleeping ear, saying, "The dark, unlovely passions you have looked upon are in your heart; watch well while they are few and weak, lest they should darken your whole life and shut out love and happiness forever. Remember well the lesson of the dream, dear child, and let the shining spirits make your heart their home."

And with that voice sounding in her ear, little Annie woke to find it was a dream. But unlike other dreams, it did not pass away, and as she sat alone, bathed in the rosy morning light, and watched the forest waken into life, she thought of the strange forms she had seen. Looking down upon the flower on her breast, she silently resolved to strive, as she had striven in her dream, to be a patient, gentle little child, to bring back light and beauty to the flower's faded leaves. And as the thought came to her mind, the flower raised its drooping head and, looking up into the earnest little face bent over it, breathed its fragrant breath to answer Annie's silent thought and strengthen her for what might come.

Meanwhile the forest was astir: birds sang their gay goodmornings from tree to tree, and leaf and flower turned to greet the sun, who rose up smiling on the world. And so beneath the forest boughs and through the dewy fields went little Annie home, better and wiser for her dreams.

Autumn flowers were dead and gone, yellow leaves lay rustling on the ground, bleak winds went whistling through the naked trees, and cold, white winter snow fell softly down. Yet now, when all looked dark and dreary, on little Annie's breast the fairy flower bloomed more beautiful than ever. The memory of her forest dream had never passed away, and through trial and temptation she had been true, and kept her resolution still unbroken. Seldom now did the warning bell sound in her ear, and seldom did the flower's fragrance cease to float about her or the fairy light to brighten all whereon it fell.

So through the long cold winter little Annie dwelt like a sunbeam in her home, each day growing richer in the love of others and happier in herself. Often was she tempted, but remembering her dream, she had only to hear the music of the fairy bell and the unkind thought or feeling would flee, the smiling spirits of gentleness and love nestled in her heart, and all was bright again.

Better and happier grew the child, fairer and sweeter grew the flower, till spring came smiling over the earth and woke the flowers, set free the streams, and welcomed back the birds. Then daily did the happy child sit among her flowers, longing for the gentle elf to come again that she might tell her gratitude for all the magic gift had done.

One day, as she sat singing in the sunny nook where all her fairest flowers bloomed, weary with gazing at the far-off sky for the little form she hoped would come, she bent to look with joyful love upon her bosom flower. And as she looked, its folded leaves spread wide apart, and rising slowly from the deep white cup appeared the smiling face of the lovely elf whose coming she had waited for so long.

"Dear Annie, look for me no longer; I am here on your own breast, for you have learned to love my gift, and it has done its work most faithfully and well," the fairy said as she looked into the happy child's bright face and laid her little arms most tenderly about her neck.

"And now have I brought another gift from Fairyland, as a fit reward for you, dear child," she said, when Annie had told all her gratitude and love. Then, touching the child with her shining wand, the fairy bid her look and listen silently.

And suddenly the world seemed changed to Annie, for the air was filled with strange, sweet sounds and all around her floated lovely forms. In every flower sat little smiling elves, singing gaily as they rocked amid the leaves. On every breeze, bright, airy spirits came floating by. Some fanned her cheek with their cool breath and waved her long hair to and fro, while others rang the flower-bells and made a pleasant rustling among the leaves. In the fountain, where the water danced and sparkled in the sun, astride of every drop she saw merry little spirits who splashed and floated in the clear, cool waves and sang as gaily as the flowers on whom they scattered glittering dew. The tall trees, whose branches rustled in the wind, sang a low, dreamy song, and the waving grass was filled with little voices she had never heard before. Butterflies whispered lovely tales in her ear and birds sang cheerful songs in a sweet language she had never understood before. Earth and air seemed filled with beauty and music she had never dreamed of until now.

"O tell me what it means, dear fairy! Is it another and lovelier dream, or is the earth in truth so beautiful as this?" she cried, looking with wondering joy upon the elf, who lay upon the flower in her breast.

"Yes, it is true, dear child," replied the fairy, "and few are the mortals to whom we give this lovely gift. What to you is now so full of music and light, to others is but a pleasant summer world; they never know the language of butterfly or bird or flower, and they are blind to all that I have given you the power to see. These fair things are your friends and playmates now, and they will teach you many pleasant lessons and give you many happy hours. The garden where you once sat weeping sad and bitter tears is now brightened by your own happiness, filled with loving friends by your own kindly thoughts and feelings, and thus rendered a pleasant summer home for the gentle, happy child whose bosom flower will never fade. And now, dear Annie, I must go; but every springtime, with the earliest flowers, will I come again to visit you and bring some fairy gift. Guard well the magic flower that I may find all fair and bright when next I come."

Then, with a kind farewell, the gentle fairy floated upward through the sunny air, smiling down upon the child until she vanished in the soft, white clouds. Little Annie stood alone in her enchanted garden, where all was brightened with the radiant light and fragrant with the perfume of her fairy flower.

Ripple, the Water Sprite

*When Sunbeam ceased, Summerwind laid down
her bowl of cherries and, from back in her acorn cup,
told this tale . . . .*

Down in the deep sea lived Ripple, a happy little water sprite. She lived in a palace of red coral, with gardens of sea flowers all round it, the waves like a blue sky above it, and white sand full of jewels for its floor. Ripple and her mates had gay times playing with the sea urchins, chasing flying fish, rocking in the shells, and weaving many-colored seaweed into delicate clothes to wear.

But the pastime Ripple loved best was to rise to the light and air, and float on the waves that rocked her softly in the sunshine while the gulls stooped to tell her news of the great world they saw in their long flights. She liked to watch little children playing on the shore, and when they ran into the sea, she caught them in her arms and held them up and kissed them, though they saw and felt only the cool water and the white foam.

Ripple had one sorrow: when tempests came and the waves rolled overhead like black clouds, ships were often wrecked, and those whom the angry sea drowned came floating down, pale and cold, to the home of the water sprites, who mourned over them and laid them in graves of white sea sand, where jewels shone like flowers.

One day a little child sank down from the storm above to the quiet that was never broken, far below. Its pretty eyes were closed as if asleep, its long hair hung about the pale face like wet weeds, and the little hands still held the shells they had been gathering when the cruel waves swept it away. The tenderhearted sprites cried salt tears over it, and wrapped it in their softest sheets, finding it so lovely and so sad that they could not bury it out of sight. While they sang their lullabies, Ripple heard through the roar of wind and water a bitter cry that seemed to call her. Floating up through foam and spray, she saw a woman standing on the beach with her arms outstretched, imploring the cruel sea to give her back her little child.

Ripple longed so much to comfort the poor mother that power was given her to show herself and to make her soft language understood. A slender creature in a robe as white as foam, with eyes as blue as the sea and a murmuring voice that made music like falling drops of water, she bent over the weeping woman and told her that the child was cared for far below all storms, and promised to keep the little grave beautiful with sea flowers and safe from any harm. But the mother could not be comforted, and still cried bitterly, "Give him back to me alive and laughing, or I cannot live. Dear sprite, have you no charm to make the little darling breathe again? Oh, find one, find one, or let me lie beside him in the hungry sea."

"I will look far and wide and see if I can help you. Watch by the shore, and I will come again with the little child if there is any power in land or sea to make him live," cried Ripple, so eager to do this happy thing that she sprang into the ocean and vanished like a bubble.

She hurried to the Queen in her palace of pearls and told her the sad story.

"Dear Ripple, you cannot keep your promise, for there is no power in my kingdom to work this spell. The only thing that could do it would be a flame from the sun to warm the little body into life, and you could never reach the fire spirits' home, for it is far, far away."

"But I *will!*" cried Ripple bravely. "If you had seen the poor mother's tears and heard her cries, you would feel as I do and never let her watch in vain. Tell me where I must go, and I will not be afraid of anything if I can only make the little child live again."

"Far away, beside the sun, live the fire spirits, but I cannot tell the road, for it is through the air, and no water sprite could live to reach it. Dear Ripple, do not go, for if any harm comes to you, I shall lose my sweetest subject," said the Queen. And all the others begged her to stay safely at home.

But Ripple would not break her promise, and they had to let her go. So the sprites built a tomb of delicate bright shells, where the child might lie till Ripple came to make him live again. With a brave goodbye Ripple floated away on her long journey to the sky.

"I will go round the world till I find a road to the sun. Some kind friend will help me, for I have no wings and cannot float through the blue air as through the sea," she said as she came to the other side of the ocean and saw a lovely land before her. Grass was green on all the hills, flowers were budding, young leaves danced upon the trees, and birds were singing everywhere.

"Why are you all so gay?" asked Ripple.

"Spring is coming! Spring is coming! And all the earth is glad," sang the lark, music pouring from its little throat.

"Shall I see her?" asked Ripple eagerly.

"You will meet her soon. The sunshine told us she was near, and we are hurrying to be up and dressed to welcome her back," answered a blue-eyed violet, dancing on her stem for joy.

"I will ask her how to reach the fire spirits. She travels over the earth every year and perhaps can show me the way," said Ripple, and continued on.

Soon a beautiful child came dancing over the hills, rosy as dawn, with hair like sunshine, a voice like the balmy wind, and her robe full of seeds, little leaves, dewdrops, and budding flowers, which she scattered far and wide, till the earth smiled back at the smiling sky.

"Dear Spring, will you help a poor little sprite who is looking for the fire spirits' home?" cried Ripple, and she told her tale so eagerly that the child stopped to hear.

"Alas, I cannot tell you," answered Spring, "but my elder sister Summer is coming behind me, and she may know. I long to help, so I will give you this breeze, which will carry you over land and sea and never tire. I wish I could do more, but the world is calling me and I must go."

"Many thanks, kind Spring," cried Ripple, as she floated away on the breeze. "Say a kind word to the poor mother waiting on the shore, and tell her I do not forget."

Then the lovely season flew on with her sunshine and song, and Ripple went swiftly over hill and dale till she came to the place where Summer lived. Here the sun shone warmly on early fruit and ripening grain; the wind blew freshly over sweet hayfields and rustled the thick branches of the trees. Heavy dews and soft showers refreshed the growing things, and long bright days brought beauty to the world.

"Now I must look for Summer," said Ripple, sailing along.

"I am here," said a voice, and she saw a beautiful woman floating by in green robes, with a golden crown on her hair and her arms full of splendid flowers.

Ripple told her story again, but Summer said with a sigh of pity, "I cannot show you the way, but my brother Autumn may know. I, too, will give you a gift to help you along, good little creature. This sunbeam will be a lamp to light your way, for you may have a gloomy journey yet."

Then Summer went on, leaving all green and golden behind her, and Ripple flew away to look for Autumn. Soon the fields were yellow with corn and grain, purple grapes hung on the vines, nuts rattled down among the dead leaves, and frost made the trees gay with lovely colors. A handsome hunter in a russet suit came striding over the hills with his hounds about him, making music on a silver horn that all the echoes answered.

This was Autumn, but he was no wiser than his sisters, and seeing the little sprite's disappointment, he kindly said, "Ask Winter; he knows the fire spirits well, for when he comes, they fly down to kindle fires on the hearths where people gather to keep warm. Take this red leaf, and when you meet his chilly winds, wrap it round you, else you will be frozen to death. A safe journey and a happy end." And with a shrill blast on his horn, Autumn hurried away, his hounds leaping after him.

"Shall I ever get there?" sighed poor Ripple as the never-tiring breeze flew on and the sky grew dark and cold winds began to blow. Then she folded the warm red leaf about her like a cloak and looked sadly down at the dead flowers and frozen fields, not knowing that Winter would spread a soft blanket of snow over them so they could lie safely asleep till Spring woke them again.

Presently, riding on the north wind, Winter came rushing by with a sparkling crown of ice in his white hair and a cloak of frost, from which he scattered snowflakes far and wide.

"What do you want with me, pretty thing? Do not be afraid; I am warm at heart, though rude and cold outside," said Winter with a smile that made his pleasant face glow in the frosty air.

When Ripple told what she was looking for, he nodded and pointed to the gloomy sky.

"Far away up there is the palace, and the only road is through cloud and mist and strange places full of danger. It is too hard a task for you, and the fire spirits are wild, hot-tempered things who may kill you. Come back with me, and do not try."

"I cannot go back, now that I have found the way. Surely the spirits will not hurt me when I tell why I have come. And if they give me the spark, I shall be the happiest sprite in all the big sea. Tell the poor mother I will keep my word, and be kind to her. She is so sad."

"You brave little creature! I think you will succeed. Take this snowflake, that will never melt, and good luck to you," cried Winter as the north wind carried him away, leaving the air full of snow.

"Now, dear breeze, fly straight up till we reach our journey's end. The sunbeam shall light the way, the red leaf shall keep me warm, and the snowflake shall lie here beside me till I need it. Goodbye to land and sea—now away, up to the sun!" When Ripple first began her airy journey, heavy clouds lay piled like hills about her and a cold mist filled the air. Higher and higher they went, and darker grew the air, while a stormy wind tossed the little traveler to and fro as if on the angry sea.

"Shall I ever see the beautiful world again?" sighed Ripple. "It is indeed a dreadful road, and but for the seasons' gifts, I should have died. Fly fast, dear wind, and bring me to the sunshine again."

Soon the clouds were left behind. The mist rolled away, and Ripple came up among the stars. With wondering eyes, she looked at the bright worlds that seemed dim and distant when she saw them from the sea. Now they moved around her, some shining with a soft light, some with many-colored rings, some pale and cold, some burning with a red glare.

Ripple would gladly have stayed to watch them, for she fancied voices called; faces smiled at her, and each star made music as it shone in the wide sky. But higher up, still nearer to the sun, she saw a far-off light that glittered like a crimson flame and made a fiery glow. "The spirits must be there," she said, and hurried on, eager to reach her journey's end.

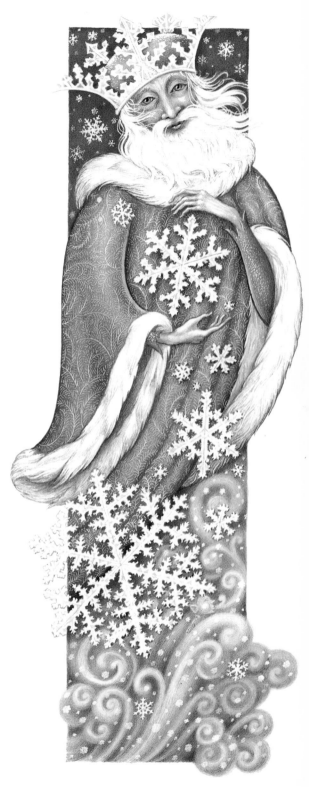

Up she flew till straight before her lay a broad path that led to a golden arch, behind which she could see lovely creatures moving to and fro. As she drew nearer, the air grew so hot that the red leaf shriveled up, and Ripple would have died if she had not quickly unfolded the snowflake and wrapped herself in its cool cloak. Then she could safely pass under the tall arch into a strange place where the walls were of orange, blue, and purple flames that made beautiful figures as they flickered to and fro. Here the fire spirits lived, and Ripple saw with wonder their crowns of flame, their flashing eyes, the sparks that popped from their lips as they spoke, and how in each one's bosom burned a little flame that never wavered or went out.

She had time to see no more, for the wild things came dancing round her, and their hot breath would have burned her if she had not pulled the snow cloak over her head. She begged them not to touch her, but to take her to the Queen.

Through the halls of many-colored fire, they led her to a spirit more brilliant than the rest. A crown of yellow flames waved on her head, and under the transparent violet of her robe, the light in her breast shone like a star.

Then Ripple told how she had been round the world to find them, and how, thanks to the seasons, she had come at last to get the magic spark that would make the little child live again.

"We cannot give it," said the Queen, "for each of us must take something from our bosom fires to make up this flame, and this we do not like to do, because the brighter these souls of ours burn, the lovelier we are."

"Dear warmhearted spirits, do not send me away without it after this long, hard journey," cried Ripple, clasping her hands. "I am sure if you do this kind thing your

souls will shine the brighter, for every good act makes us beautiful. Give me the spark and I will do anything I can for you."

As she spoke, the cloak fell back a little, and the Queen saw the chain of jewels Ripple wore.

"If you will give me those lovely blue stones that shine like water, I will give a little of my bosom fire for the child. You are a brave sprite, and it is hard to be cruel to you."

Gladly Ripple gave her the necklace, but, alas, as soon as the Queen's hand touched it, the jewels melted like snow and fell in bright drops to the ground. Then the Queen's eyes flashed and the spirits gathered angrily about Ripple, sparks showering from their lips.

"I have many finer ones at home, and if you will give me the flame, I will bring all I can gather in the sea and each shall have a necklace to remember the kind deed you have done," she said gently to the spirits hovering about her looking ready to burn her up in their wrath.

"We will do it," said the Queen. "But if the jewels you bring melt like these, we shall keep you prisoner here. Promise to come back, or we shall send lightning to find and kill you, even at the bottom of the sea."

Ripple promised, and each spirit gave a spark till the golden flame was made and put into a crystal vase, where it shone like a splendid star.

"Remember! Remember!" cried the fierce imps as they led her to the arch and left her to travel back through mist and cloud and, far below, the beautiful blue sea.

Gladly she plunged into the cool waves and sunk to her home, where her friends hastened joyfully to welcome her.

"Now come, dear, brave Ripple," they said, "and finish the good work you have begun." They gathered round the tomb, where like a marble image lay the little child.

Ripple placed the flame on his breast and watched it sparkle there while the color came slowly back to the pale face, light to the dim eyes, and breath to the cold lips, till the child woke from his long sleep and looked up smiling as he called his mother.

Then the spirits sang for joy and dressed him in clothes of woven seaweed, putting chains of shells on his neck and a wreath of water flowers on his head.

"Now you shall see your mother, who has waited so long, dear child," said Ripple, taking him in her arms and feeling that all her weariness was not in vain.

On the shore, the poor woman still sat, watching and waiting patiently, as she had done all that weary year. Suddenly a great wave came rolling in, and on it, lifted high by arms as white as foam, sat the child, waving his hands as he cried to her, "I am coming mother, and I have such lovely things to show you from the bottom of the sea!"

Then the wave broke gently on the shore and left the child safe in his happy mother's arms.

"O faithful Ripple, what can I do to thank you? I wish I had some splendid thing, but I have only this little chain of pearls. They are the tears I shed, and the sea changed them so that I might offer them to you," said the woman, when she could speak for joy.

Ripple took the pretty chain and floated away, ready for her new task, while the child danced gaily on the sand and the mother smiled like sunshine on the happy sprite who had done so much for her.

Far and wide in all the caves of the sea did Ripple look for jewels, and when she had long necklaces of all the brightest, she flew away again on the tireless breeze to the fire palace in the sky.

The spirits welcomed her warmly as she poured out her treasures at the feet of the Queen. But when the hot hands touched the jewels, they melted and fell like drops of colored dew. Ripple was filled with fear, for she could not live in that fiery place, and she begged for some other task to save her life.

"No, no," cried the spirits fiercely. "You have not kept your promise and you must stay. Fling off this cold cloak and swim in the fire fountains till you get a soul like ours and can help us brighten our bosom sparks again."

Ripple sank down in despair and felt that she must die, but even then was glad to give her life for the little child's. The spirits gathered about her, but as they began to pull the cloak away, underneath they saw the chain of pearls shining with a soft light, which only brightened as they put their hands upon it.

"Oh, give us this!" they cried. "It is finer than the others and does not melt. Give us this and you may go free."

Ripple gladly gave it and, safe under the cloak, told them how the pearls they so proudly divided to wear were tears that, but for them, would still be flowing. This pleased the spirits, for they had warm hearts as well as hot tempers, and they said, smiling, "Since we may not kiss you, and you cannot live with us, we will show our love for you by giving you a pleasant journey home. Come out and see the bright path we have made."

They led her to the gate, and there she saw a splendid rainbow arching from the sky to the sea, its lovely colors shining in the sun.

Then, with thanks and goodbyes, happy little Ripple flew back along that lovely road, and every wave in the great ocean danced for joy to welcome her home.

"Thanks, dear Summerwind," said the Queen. "We will remember the lessons you have each taught us, and when next we meet in Fern Dale, you shall tell us more. And now, dear Trip, call them from the lake, for the moon is sinking fast, and we must hasten home."

The elves gathered about their Queen, and while the rustling leaves were still, and the flowers' sweet voices mingled with their own, they sang this:

The moonlight fades from flower and tree,
And the stars dim one by one;
The tale is told, the song is sung,
And the fairy feast is done.
The night wind rocks the sleeping flowers,
And sings to them, soft and low.
The early birds erelong will wake:
'Tis time for the elves to go.

O'er the sleeping earth we silently pass,
Unseen by mortal eye,
And send sweet dreams, as we lightly float
Through the quiet moonlit sky;
For the stars' soft eyes alone may see,
And the flowers alone may know,
The feasts we hold, the tales we tell:
So 'tis time for the elves to go.

From bird, and blossom, and bee,
We learn the lessons they teach;
And seek, by kindly deeds, to win
A loving friend in each.
And though unseen on earth we dwell,
Sweet voices whisper low,
And gentle hearts most joyously greet
The elves where'er they go.

When next we meet in the fairy dell,
May the silver moon's soft light
Shine then on faces gay as now,
And elfin hearts as light.
Now spread each wing, for the eastern sky
With sunlight soon will glow.
The morning star shall light us home:
Farewell! for the elves must go.

As the music ceased, with a soft, rustling sound the elves spread their shining wings and flew silently over the sleeping earth; the flowers closed their bright eyes, the little winds were still, for the feast was over, and the fairy lessons ended. — *The End*

As the year 1855 dawned, twenty-two-year-old Louisa May Alcott penned the first entry in her new journal. "The principal event of the winter," she wrote, "is the appearance of my book 'Flower Fables.' An edition of sixteen hundred. It has sold very well, and people seem to like it. I feel quite proud that the little tales that I wrote for Ellen E[merson] when I was sixteen should now bring money and fame.... Mothers are always foolish over their first-born" (*Journals* 73). Alcott was paid $32 for *Flower Fables*—more than she had earned for the three stories and three poems she had published previously. But money was not as important as the sense of accomplishment she felt at seeing her name on the title page. She was now a published author with her own book! Alcott was indeed proud of her "first-born," and would remain so for the rest of her life. In 1886, thirty-one years after the publication of *Flower Fables*, she would jot the following comment in the margin next to her January 1, 1855 journal entry: "A pleasing contrast to the receipts of six months only in 1886, being $8000 for the sale of books, and no new one; but I was prouder over the $32 than the $8000" (*Journals* 73).

Inspired by her achievement, Alcott expressed a new-found confidence in her ability to tackle more worldly subjects. It was an optimistic daughter who tucked the small red clothbound volume into her mother's stocking on Christmas Day 1854: "Dear Mother,—Into your Christmas stocking I have put my 'first born,' knowing that you will accept it with all its faults (for grandmothers are always kind), and look upon it merely as an earnest of what I may yet do; for, with so much to cheer me on, I hope to pass in time from fairies and fables to men and

realities." She also thanked her mother for having faith in her abilities: "Whatever beauty or poetry is to be found in my little book is owing to your interest in and encouragement of all my efforts from the first to the last; and if ever I do anything to be proud of, my greatest happiness will be that I can thank you for that...." (*Selected Letters* 11).

Flower Fables became the seed for the author's productive career: more than twenty books would follow over the next three decades. But her first book would always have a special place in Alcott's memory and heart. The history behind *Flower Fables* is a fascinating one, beginning in the 1840s in the fields and forests of rural Concord, Massachusetts, and concluding some forty years later in the thriving city of Boston.

Born in 1832 in Germantown, Pennsylvania, Louisa May dreamed of becoming a writer from an early age. This was hardly surprising, since she grew up in a literary family amidst some of the most prominent authors of the day. For the Alcott children, books were, literally, toys. "One of my earliest memories," Louisa recalled, "is of playing with books in my father's study. Building towers and bridges of the big dictionaries, looking at pictures, pretending to read, and scribbling on blank pages whenever pen or pencil could be found" ("Recollections" [7]). Louisa and her three sisters were educated at home by their father, Bronson Alcott, a schoolteacher, writer, poet, and philosopher who instilled in his daughters a special love of literature. Often the family would gather to hear Bronson read aloud from John Bunyan's *Pilgrim's Progress* or listen, entranced, to their mother's rendition of a romantic novel by Sir Walter Scott (*Ivanhoe* was among their favorites). Even "the best of the dear old fairy tales made that hour the pleasantest of our day" ("Recollections" 10).

In 1845, the Alcotts moved to Concord, where Bronson could be at the center of an emerging literary movement, Transcendentalism. Here in this peaceful village, Louisa's neighbors and her family's friends included some of the most famous authors of the nineteenth century: Ralph Waldo Emerson, Henry David Thoreau, and Nathaniel Hawthorne. The young Louisa would often "venture into Mr. Emerson's library, and ask what I should read, never conscious of the audacity of my demand, so genial was my welcome." She remembered "the indulgent smile he wore when I proposed something far above my comprehension. 'Wait a little for that,' he said. 'Meantime try this; and if you like it, come again'" ("Reminiscences" 285). Bronson and his family also visited Thoreau, who would take the girls for huckleberrying parties and long walks in the Walden woods, or row them around the shoreline of Walden Pond.

While Louisa's parents and neighbors stirred her intellectual curiosity and imagination, the forests and meadows of Concord instilled in her a love and respect for nature's beauty. "My wise mother," she wrote, "anxious to give me a strong body to support a lively brain, turned me loose in the country and let me run wild, learning of nature, what no books can teach" ("Recollections" 11-12). One of these precious moments is recorded in her journal for 1845: "I had an early run in the woods before the dew was off the grass. The moss was like velvet, and as I ran under the arches of yellow and red leaves I sang for joy, my heart was so bright and the world so beautiful" (*Journals* 57).

Not only did Louisa enjoy the company of her three sisters, Anna, Elizabeth, and May, but her famous neighbors' children also became close friends, often visiting the girls at the home they named Hillside. Nathaniel Hawthorne's son, Julian, recollected the constant comings and goings among the families: "my two sisters [Rose and Una] and myself and the Alcott girls were in and out of one another's houses all the time, almost forming one family. And the three Emerson children, Ellen, Edith and Edward, being but ten minutes' distant in space and even nearer in amity, were not long in getting in the game" ("The Woman" 25). For the teenaged Louisa, the rural village seemed a paradise: "Those Concord days were the happiest of my life, for we had charming playmates in the little Emersons, [Ellery] Channings, Hawthornes...with the illustrious parents and their friends to enjoy our pranks and share our excursions" ("Recollections" 12-13).

Theatricals staged in the old Hillside barn formed a good part of their childhood fun. Louisa and her older sister, Anna, would often compose their own plays, such as "Norma, or The Witches Curse," and as Anna noted, the "greatest delight of the girls was to transform themselves into queens, knights, and cavaliers of high degree, and ascend into a world of fancy and romance" ("Foreword" 9). Edward Emerson, the oldest of Ralph Waldo Emerson's three children, also fondly recalled the plays enacted by the Alcott girls: "Love, despair, witchcraft, villainy, fairy intervention, triumphant right, held sway in turn. In those days a red scarf, long cloak, a big hat with a plume stolen from a bonnet, a paper-knife dagger,…supplemented by proper common-sense in the audience, would give castles, enchanted forests, caves and ladies' bowers" ("When Louisa" 16).

The Hillside barn also served as a schoolroom for the Emerson children, with the young Louisa as their teacher. For Ellen, the eldest daughter of the famous Concord sage, Louisa would spin adventures of nature's woodland fairies, stories inspired by her own readings and by the tales told to her by Thoreau. The icy kingdom of the Frost King would come alive for the nine-year-old Emerson girl as the brown-eyed Alcott wove her magic spell and enthralled her audience of one. At the child's insistence, Alcott finally recorded the tales in handmade books—*The Frost King* and *The Fairy Dale*—which she presented to Ellen as a gift.

Unfortunately, the idylls of Hillside came to an end when the Alcotts returned to Boston in late 1848. As Louisa worked at various jobs in the city, she also began to focus seriously on her writing. By 1854 she had published three short stories and completed her first novel, *The Inheritance,* a sentimental tale that would not be published in her lifetime. But she was already hard at work on a collection of fairy tales based on the stories originally told to Ellen Emerson. By November 1854 she had found a publisher, George W. Briggs of Boston, and *Flower Fables* appeared in December—a bit late to sell well as a Christmas present for children, the publisher's original intention.

Just the same, the book was well received. In deference to the stories' origins, Alcott dedicated the volume to her former student. That Christmas, she also sent Ellen a copy of *Flower Fables*, writing: "Hoping that age has not lessened your love for the Fairy folk I have ventured to place your name in my little book, for your interest in their sayings & doings, first called forth these 'Flower Fables,' most of which were fancied long ago in Concord woods & fields" (*Selected Letters* 10-11). The Boston *Saturday Evening Gazette* gave the book a favorable notice on December 23: "Very sweet are these little legends of Fairy land, which those of our young friends, who are so fond of tales of enchantment, will, we are sure, peruse with avidity" (2).

Alcott's work was a pioneering effort in American fantasy fiction. While a number of fairy tales had been published in the United States as early as 1785, they were mainly European in origin, such as the stories of Perrault, the Brothers Grimm, or Hans Christian Andersen. In fact, Alcott's neighbor Nathaniel Hawthorne is credited with beginning the tradition of the literary fairy tale in America with his retelling of Greek myths in *A Wonder Book* (1851) and *Tanglewood Tales* (1853). In her work, Alcott did not look to foreign lands, but to the woods and fields of her beloved Concord.

The success of *Flower Fables* buoyed the young author, and she began the spring of 1855 with dedication to her writing. In April, she recorded her plans in her journal: "I am in the garret with my papers round me, and a pile of apples to eat while I write my journal, plan stories, and enjoy the patter of rain on the roof…. I've begun to live, and have no time for sentimental musing" (*Journals* 73). She continued a steady outpouring of her tales and poems to newspapers and magazines. In 1864, she returned to the fairy tales of her youth with *The Rose Family*, a novella much like the stories of *Flower Fables.* She was now beginning to make a name for herself as an author.

Alcott was so well known by 1867 that she was offered the editorship of *Merry's Museum*, a popular children's magazine. Though she knew nothing about the job of an editor, she agreed to take on the responsibility. Not only did it provide a monthly salary, but it was another source to place her fiction. Here, she could return to the fantasy fiction of her youth. That same year she was commissioned to write "a girl's book" for Roberts Brothers publishers. By May 1868 she was reluctantly at work on her new book entitled *Little Women*: "I plod away, though I don't enjoy this sort of thing. Never liked girls or knew many, except my sisters; but our queer plays and experiences may prove interesting, though I doubt it" (*Journals* 165-166). Alcott was wrong, of course. When published in two installments in 1868-69, *Little Women* would make her fortune and secure her fame. Over the next twenty years, she became one of the most popular authors in America, especially for children. Classics such as *Little Men, Rose in Bloom, Eight Cousins,* and *Jo's Boys* would spill from her inkstand.

Alcott, however, never forgot her love of fairy tales. Fantasy fiction would continue to be a staple of her short stories. Five months before her death in March 1888, Alcott returned to her first book, *Flower Fables,* reworking five of its six tales and combining them with new ones told to her niece, Lulu. In October 1887, she published *The Frost King,* the second volume of *Lulu's Library*. Remembering her

childhood days at Hillside in Concord, she once again dedicated the new book to Ellen Emerson, "one of the good fairies." Sending Ellen a copy of the book, Alcott wrote: "I have ventured to dedicate this little book to you in memory of the happy old times when stories were told to you...." (*Selected Letters* 320). The world of Thistledown, Lilybell, and all the enchanted fairies of the woodlands came alive once again for new readers. In one of her last books, Alcott had traced the round again, coming full circle to her first-born.

Alcott, Louisa May. Dedication page. *Lulu's Library,* vol. 2, *The Frost King*. Boston: Roberts Brothers, 1887.

—. *The Journals of Louisa May Alcott.* Edited by Joel Myerson, Daniel Shealy, and Madeleine B. Stern. Boston: Little, Brown, 1989.

—. "Recollections of My Childhood." In *Lulu's Library,* vol. 3, *Recollections*. Boston: Roberts Brothers, 1890, pp. [7]-21.

—. "Reminiscences of Ralph Waldo Emerson." In *Some Noted Princes, Authors, and Statesmen of Our Time.* Edited by James Parton. New York: Thomas Y. Crowell, 1885, pp. 284-288.

—. *The Selected Letters of Louisa May Alcott.* Edited by Joel Myerson, Daniel Shealy, and Madeleine B. Stern. Boston: Little, Brown, 1987.

Emerson, Edward. "When Louisa Alcott Was a Girl." *Ladies Home Journal* (December 1898): 16-18.

Hawthorne, Julian. "The Woman Who Wrote Little Women." *Ladies Home Journal* (October 1922): 25, 120-124.

Pratt, Anna Alcott. "A Foreword by Meg." In *Comic Tragedies: Written by "Jo" and "Meg," and Acted by the "Little Women."* Boston: Roberts Brothers, 1893, pp. [7]-13.

Saturday Evening Gazette (Boston), 23 December 1854, p. [2].

Biographies

Louisa May Alcott's life and work were shaped by numerous influences, and within the intellectual orbit of her family, certain writers, philosophers, and public figures were held in high esteem. Hidden in the illustrations throughout this book are quotes from and miniature portraits of some of these figures, as well as Alcott herself. The following biographies are the luminaries to be found by the diligent detective.

LOUISA MAY ALCOTT (1832-1888), author of over twenty books and three hundred stories and articles, once declared, "I wish I had a fuller record to offer." Having held jobs as a teacher, governess, seamstress, Civil War nurse, and domestic servant, Alcott turned to writing to support what she nicknamed "the Pathetic Family." Alcott's *Little Women* series made her one of the best-selling writers of the nineteenth century.

ABIGAIL ALCOTT (1800-1877), daughter of a prominent Boston merchant, married Bronson Alcott in 1830. A fervent abolitionist and proponent of women's rights, Abby served as a model for Jo's beloved Marmee in *Little Women*. Alcott once confessed in her journal, "All the philosophy in our house is not in the study; a good deal is in the kitchen, where a fine old lady thinks high thoughts and does kind deeds while she cooks and scrubs."

BRONSON ALCOTT (1799-1888), philosopher, poet, and author, was born a poor Connecticut farmer. In 1834, he opened the progressive Temple School in Boston. After its closure in 1839, Bronson, an important figure in the Transcendentalist movement, turned to giving "conversations," or lectures, in private homes. About her father's childhood, Louisa once said, "I never realized so plainly before how much he has done for himself."

CHARLOTTE BRONTE (1816-1855), author of *Jane Eyre,* was among Alcott's favorite writers as a child.

JOHN BUNYAN (1628-1688), Puritan minister and writer, was most famous for his allegory *The Pilgrim's Progress*, a perennial favorite in the Alcott household.

CHARLES DICKENS (1812-1870), popular British novelist and author of such classic works as *Oliver Twist* and *Great Expectations*. The Alcott sisters' family newspaper, "The Pickwick Portfolio," was based on Dickens's novel *The Pickwick Papers*. In 1867, Alcott published "A Dickens Day," which recorded her tour of London, especially those locales associated with Dickens's novels.

RALPH WALDO EMERSON (1803-1882), American writer, lecturer, and poet, best known for his essays "Self-Reliance," "The American Scholar," and *Nature*. A leader of the Transcendentalist movement, Emerson was a neighbor and close friend of the Alcott family. Calling Emerson "my Master," Alcott once remarked that knowing the famous writer was "the greatest honor and happiness of my life."

MARGARET FULLER (1810-1850), teacher, author, and Transcendentalist known for her feminist work, *Woman in the Nineteenth Century*. Fuller assisted Bronson Alcott at his Temple School.

JOHANN WOLFGANG VON GOETHE (1749-1832), German Romantic writer and poet who greatly influenced American Romanticism. Alcott was introduced to his work by Emerson and, as late as 1888, claimed that Goethe "is still my favorite author."

NATHANIEL HAWTHORNE (1804-1864), author of the classic American novels *The Scarlet Letter* and *The House of the Seven Gables*, purchased the Alcott home, Hillside, in 1852, renaming it The Wayside. Five years later, the Alcotts moved into Orchard House, next door to Hawthorne. Louisa often cited Hawthorne as one of her favorite authors, and was close friends with his three children.

ABRAHAM LINCOLN (1809-1865), sixteenth president of the United States from 1861 until his assassination in April 1865. Upon hearing of the president's death, Alcott wrote that the city of Boston "went into mourning. I am glad to have seen such a strange & sudden change in the nation's feelings."

PLATO (ca. 428-348 BC), Greek philosopher whose ideas had a profound influence on Bronson Alcott's philosophy. Emerson once remarked that Bronson "could have talked with Plato."

WILLIAM SHAKESPEARE (1564-1616), British poet and playwright, most famous for such plays as *Hamlet*, *King Lear*, and *Romeo and Juliet*. Alcott enjoyed attending contemporary performances of Shakespeare's plays in Boston and New York.

SOCRATES (ca. 470-399 BC), Greek philosopher whose method of instruction, a series of interrogations referred to as the Socratic method, influenced Bronson Alcott's teaching style.

HENRY DAVID THOREAU (1817-1862), poet, naturalist, and author, best known for his 1854 *Walden*, remained a great friend of the Alcott family. Upon his death in 1862, Louisa said that "though his life seemed too short, it would blossom & bear fruit…long after he was gone." In September 1863, she honored her departed friend by publishing her poem "Thoreau's Flute" in the *Atlantic Monthly*.

HARRIET ROSS TUBMAN (1820-1913), herself a slave until she escaped via the Underground Railroad in 1849, became a conductor of the Railroad, bringing more than 3,000 to freedom, including her sisters and brother. Known among slaves as "Moses," Tubman was also an advocate for the homeless and for women's rights.

WILLIAM WORDSWORTH (1770-1850), British Romantic poet, best known for his poems set in the Lake country of England. Wordsworth greatly influenced the Transcendentalists, especially Emerson.

Acknowledgments and Credits

Many people offered encouragement and advice in the realization of *Flower Fables,* and I can only hope that others will embrace this book with equal enthusiasm. My gratitude and love to the angels who helped spark Okey-Doke Productions and this project: Edward and Shirley Giel, Tom and Judy Giel, Tom and Diane Tessman, Lenny Leaman, and Christine Carter, the guardian angel of this book. A thousand thanks to Daniel Shealy for bringing Alcott's delightful fairy tales to light, and to Leah Palmer Preiss for bringing them to visual life (Louisa would be pleased). Their unwavering commitment to this project kept it alive throughout the years. The stellar talents of Rymn Massand, Naomi Mizusaki, and Susan Chun contributed tenfold to the book's beauty. I am indebted in inexpressible ways to my marvelous family: my father, who introduced me to the world of books; my mother, one of the most beautiful women I know; my sisters and brother, Debra, Tom, Susie, and Lori, just the thought of whom gives me joy. Many friends kept me afloat with humor and affection during some trying moments, especially Howard Childs and Kathi Scharer. Doris Bry and Gene Winick contributed their wisdom and impeccable views toward work and life. Finally, thanks to Charlie Melcher, for reconnecting.—Kate

Thank you to my family—constant counselors, Kathleen, Karen, John, and Dale—you are the cycle of life to me; my nieces and nephew, Rachel, Maddie and Ian, without you I might have missed this fairy sighting. To my business partner, Kate, whose gift with books has come blessedly my way. And to Betty Burnham and all of you who recognized and encouraged the vision of this work.—Christine

My heartfelt thanks to Elliot Offner—for remembrance. To Kate, for believing in fairies and believing in me. And to Tony, Alex, and James, for gallantry and heroism when I was lost in Fairyland.—Leah

I would like to acknowledge the patience, support, and love that my wife, Margaret, has shown throughout this project—she never refused to listen to the numerous stories about Alcott and her fairy tales.—Daniel

Flower Fables was produced and published by Okey-Doke Productions, Inc.

Kate Giel, publisher and editorial director
Christine Carter, associate publisher and marketing director
Susan Chun, production director
Rymn Massand and Naomi Mizusaki, designers
Philomena Mariani and David Terrien, copyeditors

The illustrations were created primarily in watercolor, with some gouache and colored pencil, on Arches hot-pressed watercolor paper. All of the illustrations are reproduced at actual size. The typeface is Mrs. Eaves. The four-color film was produced by Professional Graphics, Rockford, Illinois, under the direction of Pat Goley and Cyndi Richards. The book is printed on Gardapat art paper by Mondadori Printing Company, Toledo, Spain, under the direction of Nancy Freeman, Angel Herrera, and Paolo Veronesi.